DRACULA MARRIES FRANKENSTEIN!

an
ANNE of GREEN BAGELS
story

PAPERCUTZ

For Bram and Mary, with special thanks to John P. Stratton

DRACULA MARRIES FRANKENSTEIN!

Susan Schade • Jon Buller

an *ANNE* of *GREEN BAGELS* story

I'M NEVER MAKING ANOTHER FILM.

PAPERCUTZ

New York

DRACULA MARRIES FRANKENSTEIN!
An Anne of Green Bagels Story
Created by Jon Buller and Susan Schade
Jeff Whitman — Editor
Jim Salicrup
Editor-in-Chief

ISBN: 978-1-62991-815-0

Printed in China
October 2017

Papercutz books may be purchased for business or promotional use.

For information on bulk purchases please contact Macmillan Corporate and Premium Sales Department at (800) 221-7945 x5442.

Distributed by Macmillan
First Printing

1

CREATURES OF
THE NIGHT

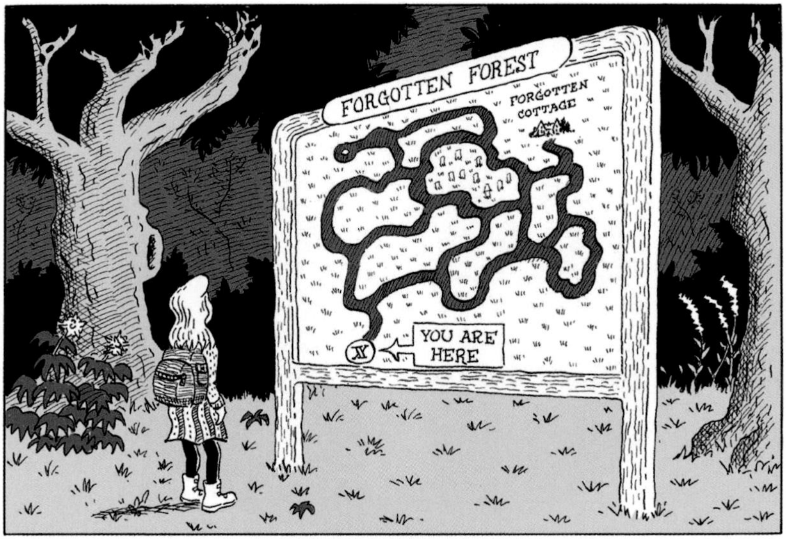
FORGOTTEN FOREST
FORGOTTEN COTTAGE
YOU ARE HERE

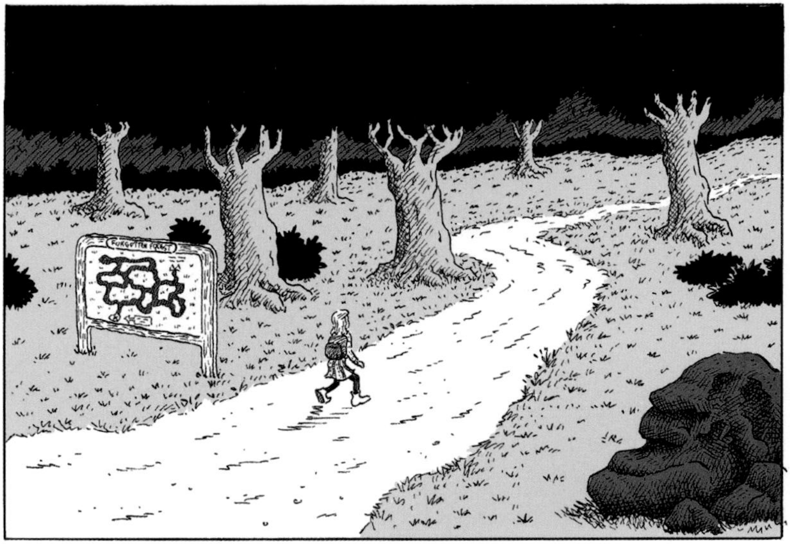

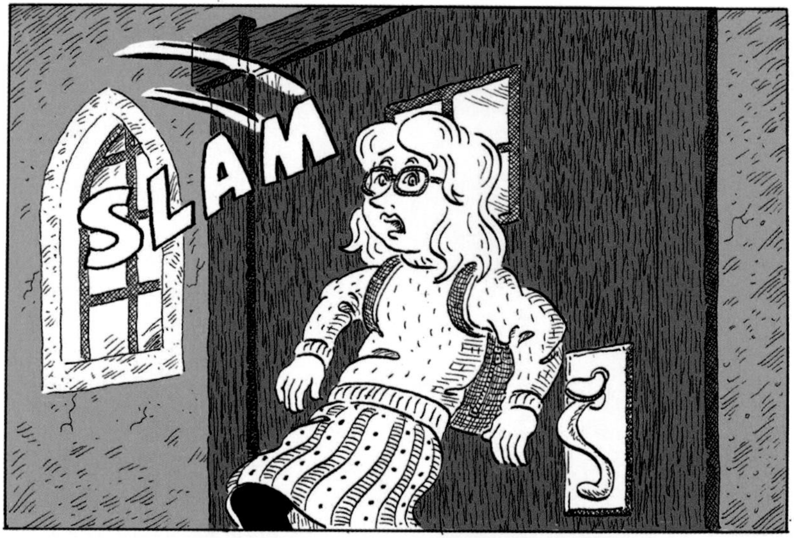
SLAM

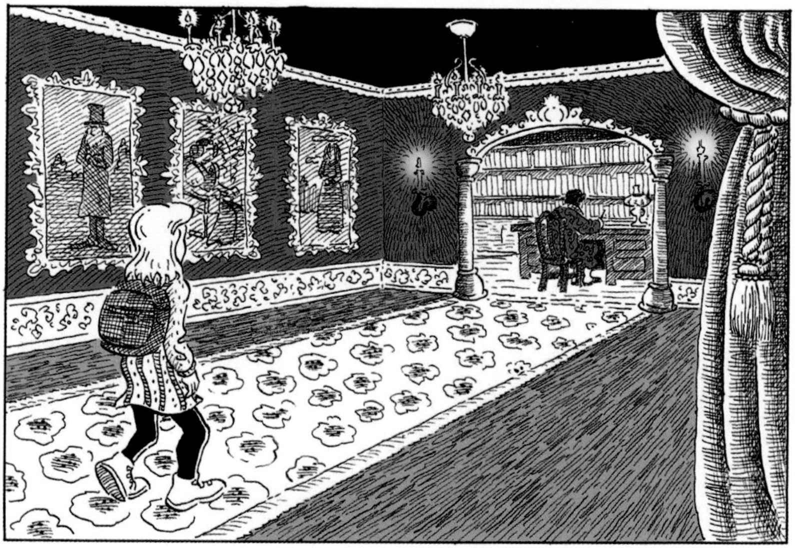

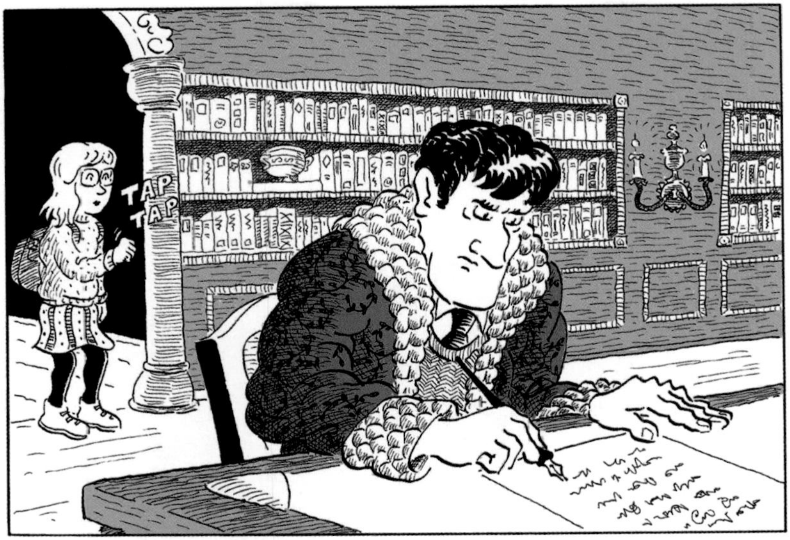
TAP
TAP

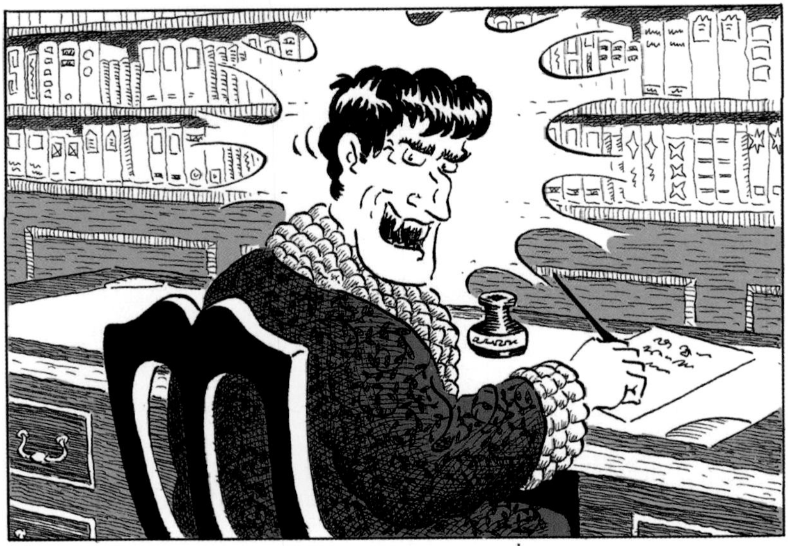

2

HERRINGBONE
HALL

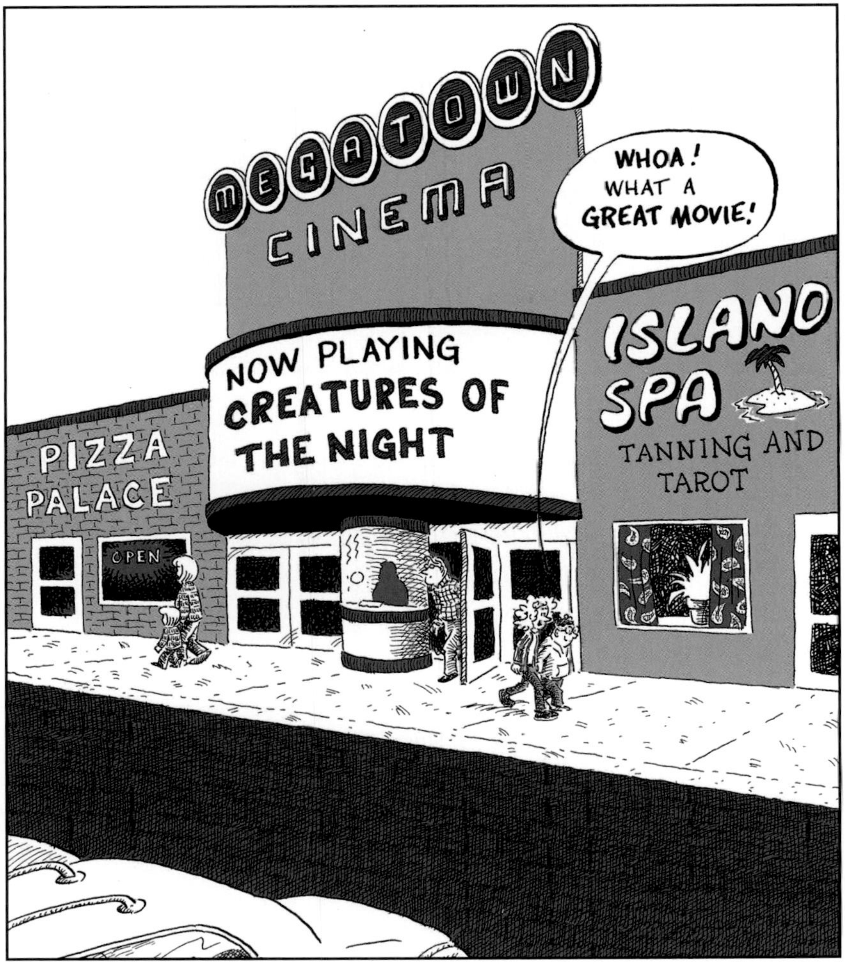
MEGATOWN
CINEMA
WHOA! WHAT A GREAT MOVIE!
NOW PLAYING
CREATURES OF THE NIGHT
PIZZA PALACE
OPEN
ISLAND SPA
TANNING AND TAROT

Now that I'm older, I love being scared, especially if I know there's going to be a happy ending afterwards. My friend Otto liked the movie too.

I LIKED THE PART WHERE THE LADY DIDN'T REALIZE DRACULA'S ASHES WERE HIDDEN IN HER JAR OF INSTANT COFFEE.
RIGHT. AND THEN WHEN SHE MAKES A CUP OF COFFEE — **WHOOSH** - OUT HE COMES!

We live in Megatown. It is supposed to be a "model community." When it was first built, all the houses were almost exactly the same. Now, thanks to my dad fighting City Hall, some of them have additions like porches and stuff.

Megatown Cinema is in the shopping center on Megatown Turnpike. It was a nice day. Otto and I decided to walk home the long way.

I said, "I'd like to be a movie director when I grow up."

"Not me," said Otto. "I could do the soundtrack, though. That would be cool. Would you hire me?"

"Sure, as long as I had the final say."

We crossed Daffodil Lane and walked along Airport Road for a while.

"We could play the music ourselves," I said, dreaming about our movie careers. "The Green Bagels, I mean." (That's our band — we play in school programs and stuff, and sometimes post our videos on YouTube.)

"I know," said Otto. "If we're still together."

Not together? I didn't like thinking about that. We had put a lot of work into developing our own unique sound — Brendan Boyle on electric guitar, me on fiddle, Otto on accordion, and the twins on vocals.

"You know what?" he said. "We could make a movie now!"

"Now? You mean this summer?"

"Sure. We already make our music videos on our cameras, don't we?"

"Yeah, but a whole movie? With actors and editing and special effects and everything?"

"Why not? We can learn. My mom could help us and she's got all the software we would need. She could show us how to make it look like you're coming out of the coffee cup."

HEY, HOLD ON! I AM **NOT** PLAYING **DRACULA!**

Otto laughed. "Just kidding," he said. "We wouldn't want to copy *Creatures of the Night* anyway."

Could we really make a movie? I was liking the idea a lot. I would be the director, of course.

"Still," said Otto, "I think it should be a horror movie."

I stopped and looked at him.

"Don't you?" he added.

"You're going too fast," I said. "We need a story, a location, actors, a script … "

"Fine!" said Otto. "Let's start with location. We have to film around here. I mean, we're not going to be able to travel to Transylvania or anything."

"But who would set a horror movie in Megatown? There's nothing scary about Megatown."

"Haha! You thought it was pretty scary when you first moved here, with the houses all the same and the streets like a giant maze."

"Well, the houses aren't all the same any more, and besides, I've gotten used to it."

Without even noticing it we had walked to a part of Megatown where all the street names were strange to me.

"I've never been this far before," I said to Otto.

Otto is a native. He knows everything about Megatown.

"You haven't?" he said. "Well, here's something really interesting. You see that big

16

house at the end of the street that's different from all the Megatown houses around it? That's Herringbone Hall."

"The Herringbone family owned all the land around here before they sold it to Norbert Meggett, the guy who built Megatown. They only kept Herringbone Hall and the lot it stands on."

I looked at the pile of towers and turrets silhouetted against the afternoon sky. "It's huge," I said.

"Yeah, and now there's just one Herringbone left — Augusta, her name is. They say she hates Megatown, and keeps all her curtains closed so she doesn't have to look at it."

"Wow," I said. "Creepy."

"Yeah, I wouldn't go near there if you paid me."

"Just the place to film a horror movie," I said slowly.

"What? Oh, no. Forget that!"

"Let's ask her," I said, and started walking towards Herringbone Hall.

HEY, WHO WANTS TO MAKE A HORROR MOVIE ANYWAY? HOW ABOUT A COMEDY? OR A MYSTERY? OR...
OH, CRUD.

3

MR. ROCK SPEAKS

RINNG
BELL
I DON'T THINK ANYONE'S HOME. LET'S GO.
LET'S GIVE IT ONE MORE TRY.
KLOMP KLOMP KLOMP
UH-OH...
KREEEK

WHAT?
BELL
OH... HI! MY NAME IS ANNE, AND THIS IS MY FRIEND, OTTO. WE WANTED TO KNOW IF IT WOULD BE OKAY TO USE YOUR HOUSE AS A LOCATION FOR OUR MOVIE.
YOU COME.
WAIT HERE.

ANNE, DO YOU REMEMBER HOW TO GET OUT OF HERE IF WE HAVE TO MAKE A RUN FOR IT?
Visitors, Gregory?
We don't usually have visitors. They frighten the squirrels.
YES, I SEE YOU HAVE A LOT OF SQUIRRELS. YOU MUST REALLY LIKE SQUIRRELS.
Well, they can be a nuisance, but they're better than people! Now please have a seat and tell me why you're here.
WE WANT TO MAKE A MOVIE ABOUT VAMPIRES, AND WE NEED A HOUSE THAT LOOKS REALLY...UH... INTERESTING, FOR BACKGROUNDS AND STUFF.

I suppose we could discuss it.
YOU WOULDN'T HAVE TO WORRY ABOUT US MAKING A MESS. WE WOULD CLEAN UP EVERYTHING.
Excuse me, dears. I didn't mean I could discuss it with you!
It's something I would like to discuss with my little mineral friends.
DO YOU MEAN THESE ROCKS THAT ARE ALL OVER THE PLACE? THEY ALL LOOK LIKE THEY HAVE FACES!
Yes, that is what drew me to them at first. But I soon found out that they have voices as well.

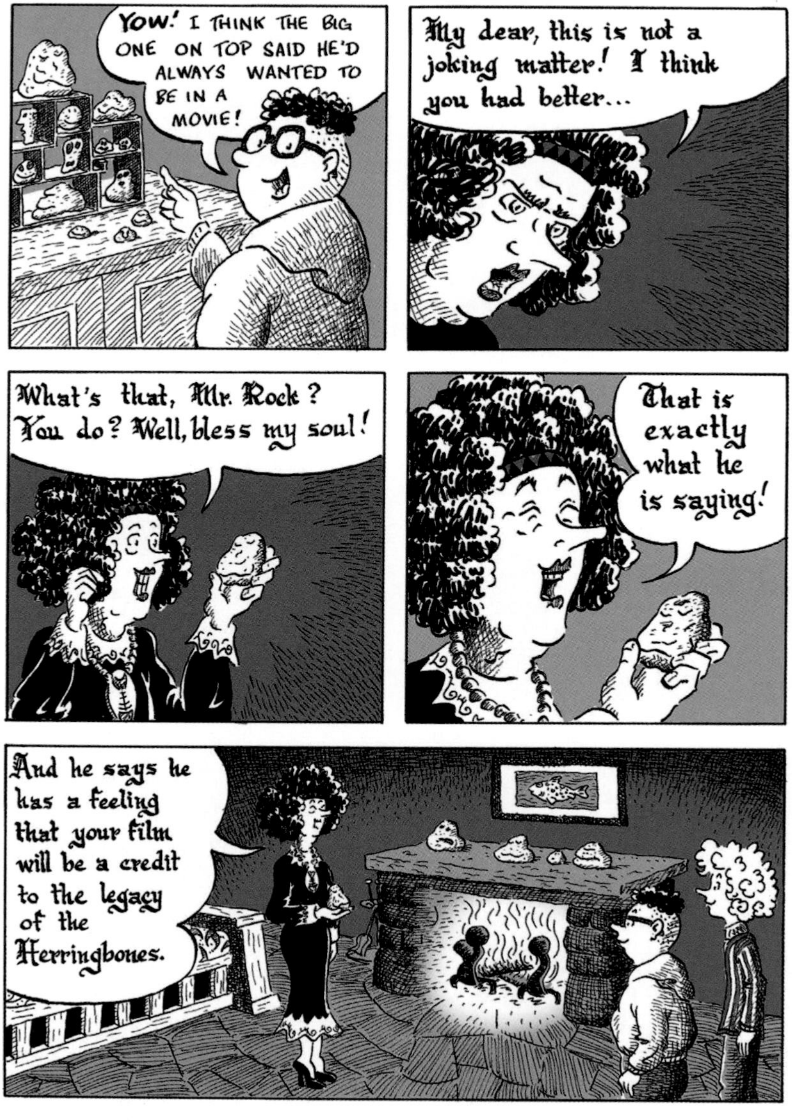
YOW! I THINK THE BIG ONE ON TOP SAID HE'D ALWAYS WANTED TO BE IN A MOVIE!
My dear, this is not a joking matter! I think you had better...
What's that, Mr. Rock? You do? Well, bless my soul!
That is exactly what he is saying!
And he says he has a feeling that your film will be a credit to the legacy of the Herringbones.

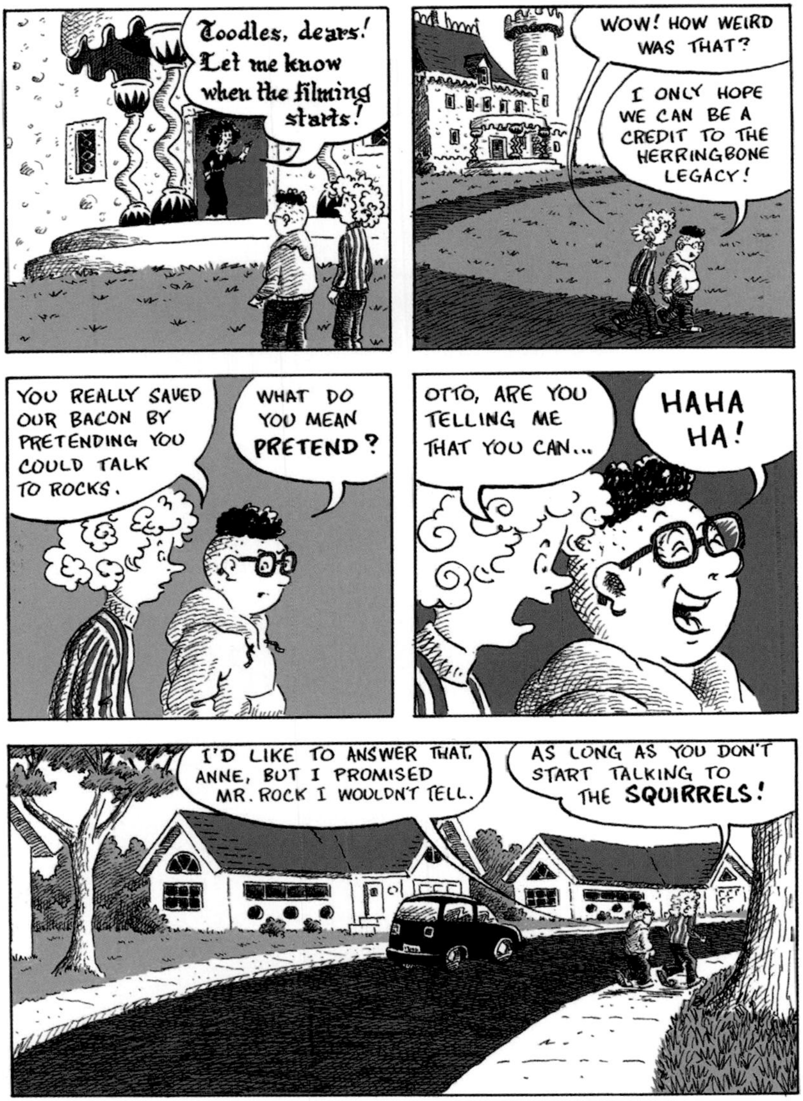
Toodles, dears! Let me know when the filming starts!
WOW! HOW WEIRD WAS THAT?
I ONLY HOPE WE CAN BE A CREDIT TO THE HERRINGBONE LEGACY!
YOU REALLY SAVED OUR BACON BY PRETENDING YOU COULD TALK TO ROCKS.
WHAT DO YOU MEAN PRETEND?
OTTO, ARE YOU TELLING ME THAT YOU CAN...
HAHA HA!
I'D LIKE TO ANSWER THAT, ANNE, BUT I PROMISED MR. ROCK I WOULDN'T TELL.
AS LONG AS YOU DON'T START TALKING TO THE SQUIRRELS!

4

BACKYARD
PROJECTS

"Hey, Dad!" I yelled when I got home. "Guess what?"

My dad is always working on some oddball project. Just then he was out in the backyard welding something on his mini-sub.

He turned off his welding torch, pushed up his face guard, and looked at me seriously. "You just got accepted into MIT? And you get to skip high school?"

"Oh, Dad, don't be silly. Me and Otto are making a movie!"

"Otto and I," Dad corrected automatically. "Good idea." He pulled down his face guard and turned on the torch.

I went inside and asked Nana if I could have some rice crackers and cheese for Dad and me. Because that's the best way to get him to listen.

We sat in the rock garden and ate our snack. "Do you think that rock has a face?" I asked him.

He looked at the same rock. "No, but it has a butt crack. I guess its pants are slipping."

I ignored that. "Augusta Herringbone has a collection of rocks with faces," I said.

"Augusta Herringbone!" That got his attention. "Don't tell me you know Augusta Herringbone! I've been trying to get a meeting with her for months."

"We went to her house today — me and Otto — I mean, Otto and I," I added quickly. "She's letting us film our movie there. It's a horror movie, and her house is really creepy, and she has this butler called Gregory, and she's got a whole collection of rocks that have faces, and she talks to them, and she thinks they talk back. Plus she has a lot of squirrels. Live-in ones, I mean. And her house smells funny."

Dad had stopped eating and was gaping at me. But all he said was, "I should think so, if her house is full of live squirrels.

"Augusta Herringbone ..." he continued. "Maybe you can introduce me. Do you know she owns a stretch of property on the waterfront?"

Dad is especially interested in waterfront property right now. Well, actually in water property, because he's working with the Oceanographic College on this underwater lab project. In fact, I happen to know that the mini-sub he's working on in our yard right now is for travelling back and forth to the underwater lab.

Dad got up and gave the mini-sub a fond pat on the side.

I could tell our movie discussion was over for the time being. Already he was staring past me with that unfocused look he gets sometimes.

What was he seeing? I wondered. A seaweed forest? A whole village of coral houses under the sea? People in mini-subs commuting to work? Would his dreams ever come true?

I went back inside. I was having some dreams of my own. Eerie music — DON DA DON ... period costumes? ...the audience enthralled, on the edges of their seats, goosebumps on the back of their necks ...oooeeeoooeee on the violin. Then BLAM! THE MONSTROUS SHAPE REARS UP! That FACE! AAUGH! SCREAMS! GASPS!

"Anne, whatever is the matter?!"
I guess I was making a scary face or something.
"Nothing, Mom, I'm fine."

5

SEAWEED PIE

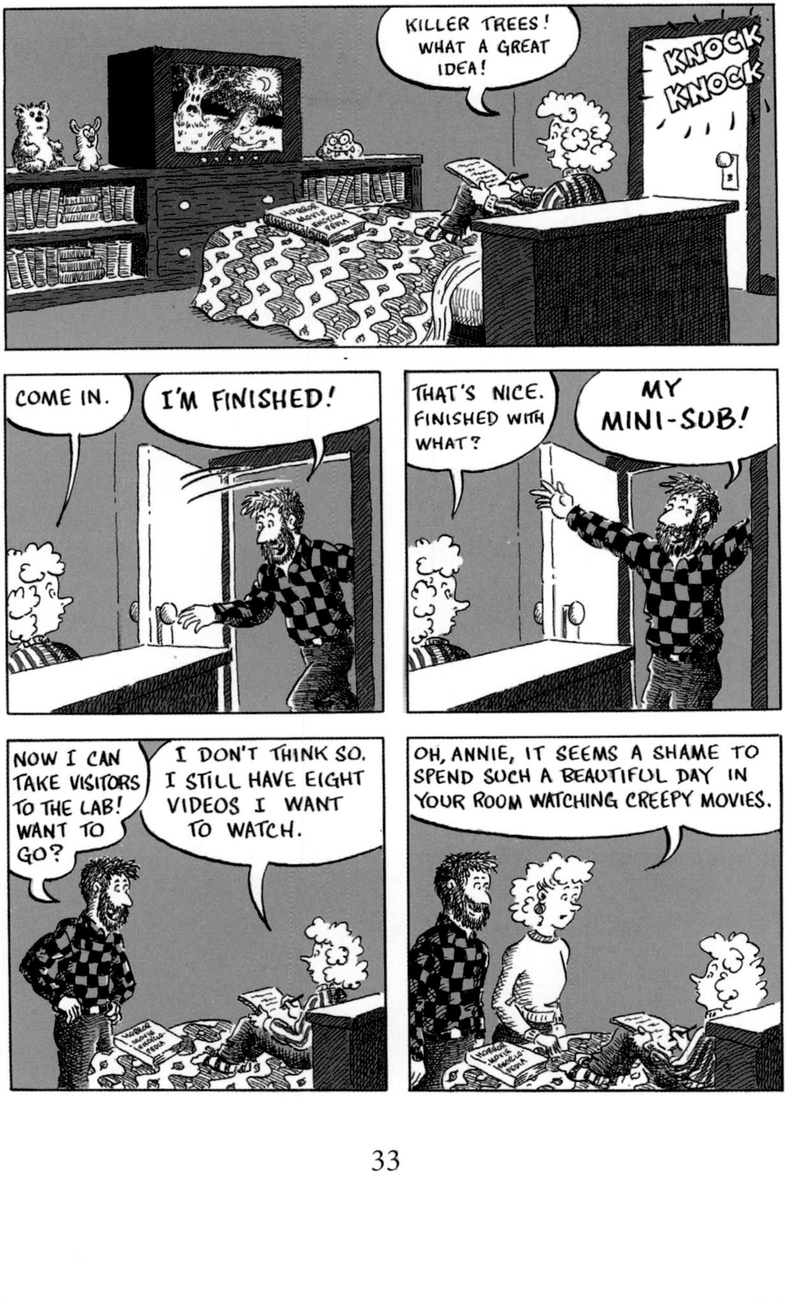
KILLER TREES! WHAT A GREAT IDEA!
KNOCK KNOCK
COME IN.
I'M FINISHED!
THAT'S NICE. FINISHED WITH WHAT?
MY MINI-SUB!
NOW I CAN TAKE VISITORS TO THE LAB! WANT TO GO?
I DON'T THINK SO. I STILL HAVE EIGHT VIDEOS I WANT TO WATCH.
OH, ANNIE, IT SEEMS A SHAME TO SPEND SUCH A BEAUTIFUL DAY IN YOUR ROOM WATCHING CREEPY MOVIES.

EXACTLY! LET'S ALL THREE OF US GO TO THE LAB!
ARE YOU SURE IT'S SAFE?
ABSOLUTELY! I'VE GOT TWO EXTRA ROLLS OF DUCT TAPE!
IT'S NOT SOMETHING TO JOKE ABOUT, ROSS.
BUT I WOULD REALLY LIKE TO SEE THIS LAB I'VE HEARD SO MUCH ABOUT.
YOU CAN BARELY HEAR THE SEAWATER-FUSION ENGINE.
MMMMMMMMMM
ANCHORS AWEIGH!

WE'RE LIVING IN CRITICAL TIMES, ANNIE.
A FEW BILLION YEARS AGO, CREATURES FROM THE SEA BEGAN LIVING ON THE LAND.
WE ARE THE DESCENDANTS OF THOSE CREATURES, AND WE HAVE DONE A GREAT JOB OF MESSING UP THAT LAND.
!
NOW I THINK IT'S TIME THAT WE WENT BACK TO WHERE WE CAME FROM!

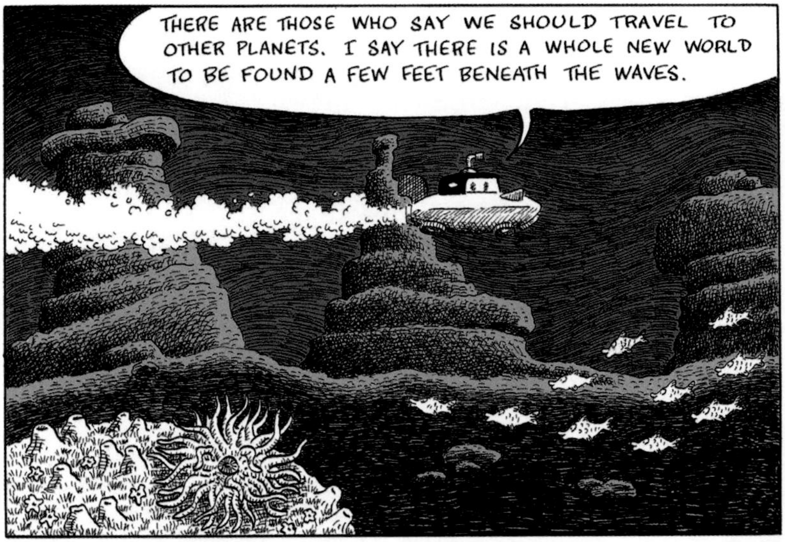
THERE ARE THOSE WHO SAY WE SHOULD TRAVEL TO OTHER PLANETS. I SAY THERE IS A WHOLE NEW WORLD TO BE FOUND A FEW FEET BENEATH THE WAVES.

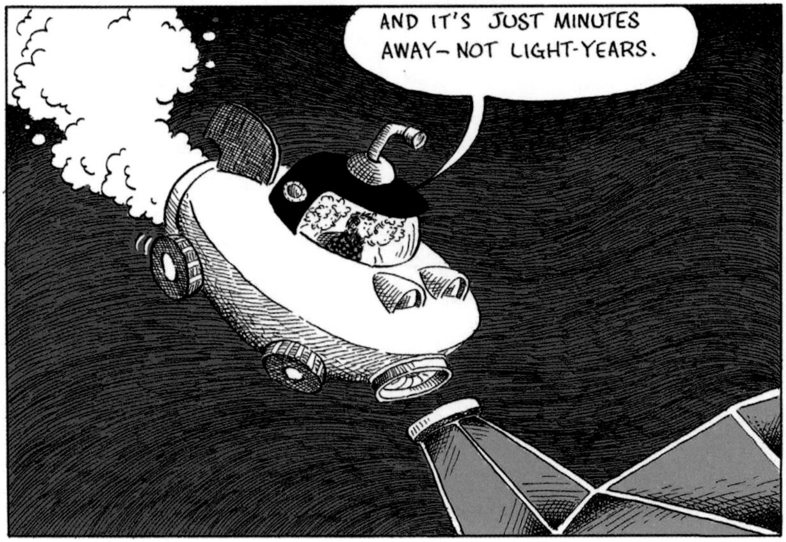
AND IT'S JUST MINUTES AWAY– NOT LIGHT-YEARS.

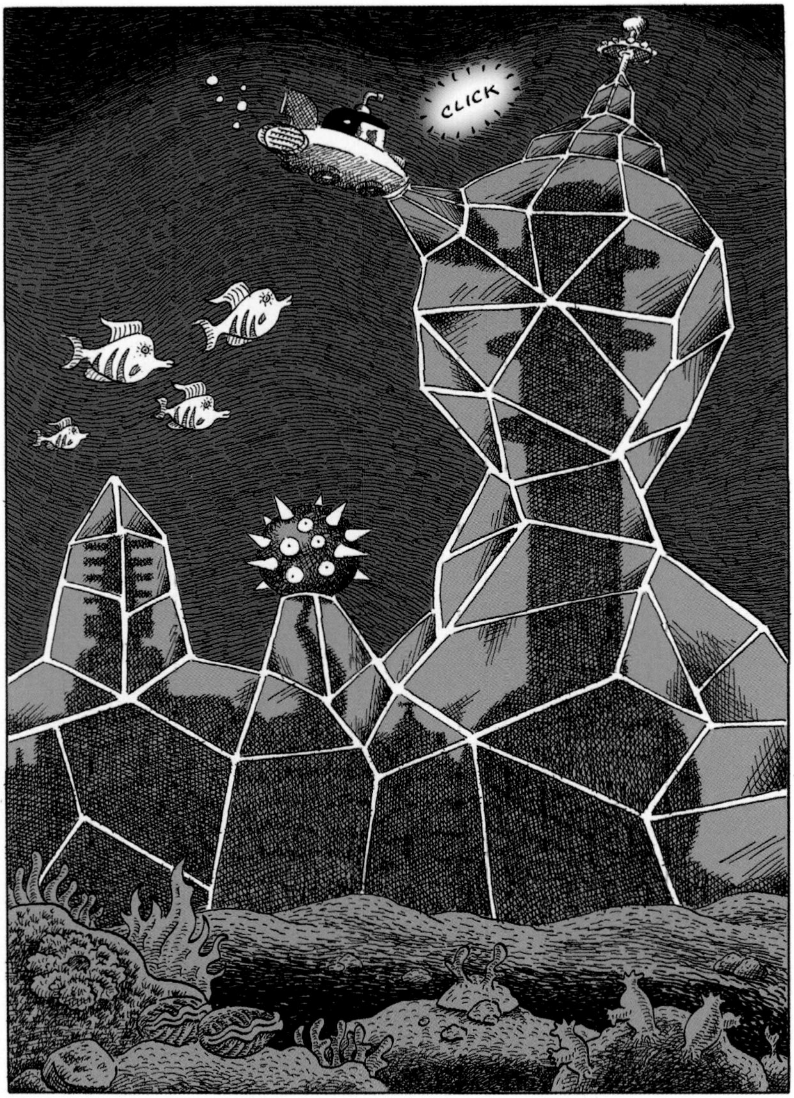
CLICK

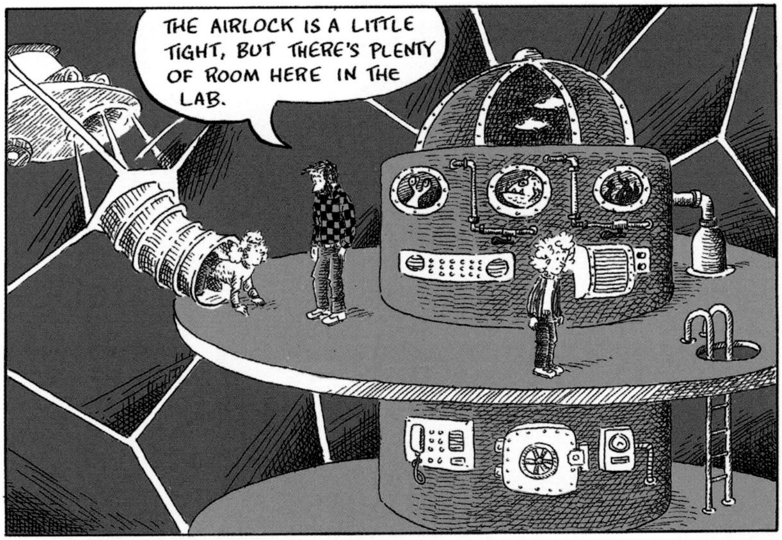
THE AIRLOCK IS A LITTLE TIGHT, BUT THERE'S PLENTY OF ROOM HERE IN THE LAB.

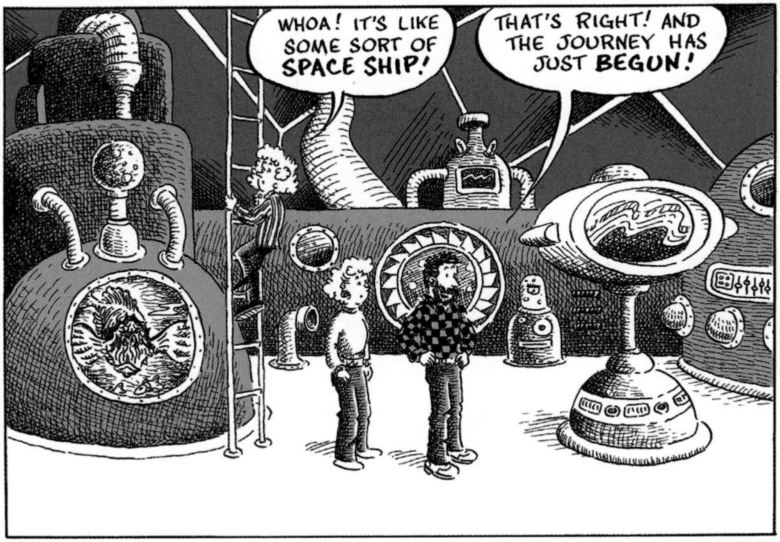
WHOA! IT'S LIKE SOME SORT OF **SPACE SHIP**!
THAT'S RIGHT! AND THE JOURNEY HAS JUST **BEGUN**!

BUT ARE YOU REALLY SERIOUS ABOUT LOTS OF PEOPLE LIVING IN THE SEA?
ABSOLUTELY! THE SEA PROVIDES EVERYTHING WE NEED!
EVERYTHING?
WAIT HERE A SECOND. I'LL BE RIGHT BACK.
HERE, TRY A SLICE OF THIS!
WHAT IS IT?
SEAWEED PIE!
MMM. ACTUALLY, IT'S NOT BAD.

6

GARAGE PLAN

The next day we held a meeting of the band in Otto's garage.

"I saw your dad's mini-sub going down Rose Lane yesterday," Brendan Boyle said to me. Last winter he would have added some rude remark about dad playing with his toys again, but now we were friends.

"Yeah," I said, "he took me and Mom to see the underwater lab."

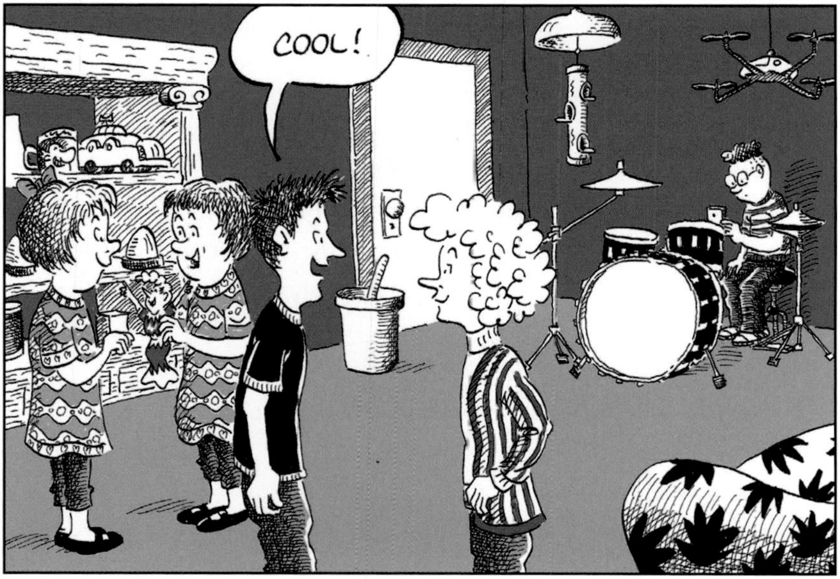
COOL!

"Cool, but that's not what we came here for today," said Otto in a getting-down-to-business voice, sitting at his old drum set.

"Do we have a gig?" asked Poppy.

"We can't sing this Saturday," said her twin, Paula. "We're going to see *Shakespeare in the Park* or something."

"It's not a gig," said Otto. "It's a ..." (and he gave a drumroll and a cymbal clash) "... MOVIE!"

"Movie? What movie?" asked Brendan

"When is it?" asked Poppy and Paula together, like two backup singers.

"No, no," said Otto. "We're not going to a movie. We're making a movie. This summer. You tell them, Anne."

"Okay, so we saw *Creatures of the Night*, and ..."

"Cool. I saw it Tuesday."

"We aren't planning on going."

"... AND we thought, 'Why don't we make a movie?' And we already have a location for it — HERRINGBONE HALL! So we thought that would be a good spot for a HORROR MOVIE. And I'm the director, and Otto is in charge of the soundtrack, which we (The Green Bagels) would play, and you guys can be in it. What do you think?"

"A horror movie? But we don't really like horror movies."

Paula said she agreed with Poppy. "We like funny movies. Or romantic movies. Or funny and romantic movies. We like movies that end with a wedding."

"Ha ha," laughed Brendan. "No problem. The girl can marry the monster at the end. I'll be the monster."

"Or the monsters can marry each other," laughed Otto. "Like *Godzilla Meets Frankenstein* — only it would be *Godzilla Marries Frankenstein!*"

"Except I've always wanted to be Dracula," said Brendan, showing his teeth and leering at Paula.

42

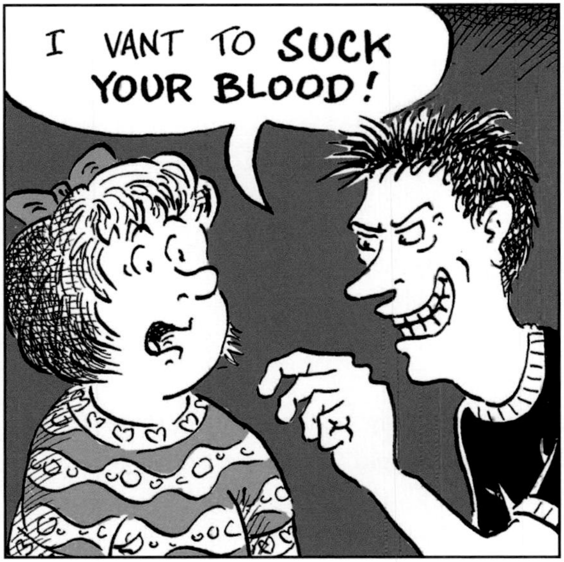
I VANT TO SUCK YOUR BLOOD!

"I guess it would be funny, at least," said Paula.

"Could we have costumes?" asked Poppy. "Regency period, maybe, but tattered and torn. We have a big dress-up chest, don't we Paula? We could do costumes."

"Okay, great!" I jumped off my stool and pulled my tablet out of my backpack.

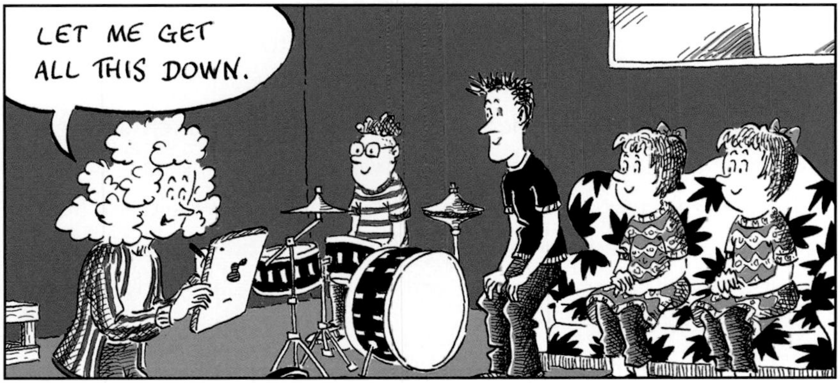
LET ME GET ALL THIS DOWN.

I started to write —
TITLE: Dracula Marries Frankenstein
DIRECTOR: Anne Blossom
SCRIPT: Anne Blossom
SCORE: Otto Immaculata
MUSIC: The Green Bagels
COSTUMES: Paula and Poppy Kubitsky
LOCATION: Herringbone Hall
ACTORS: Dracula — Brendan Boyle
                Frankenstein —

"We'll have to find someone to play Frankenstein," I said. "And what about the other characters? Should we have a pretty girl?"

"Absolutely," said Brendan.

"ZOMBIES!" said Paula, suddenly getting into it. "I think we should have zombies!"

"Oh, yuck, Paula," said Poppy.

"What? I think zombies are sort of cute."

"Speaking of cute," I said, "There are a lot of squirrels in Herringbone Hall. I wonder if any of them are trained."

"Don't forget the talking rocks," added Otto.

"What talking rocks?" everyone wanted to know.

So we had to explain the talking rocks and the squirrels and Augusta Herringbone. And after that it was time to go home.

I promised to write the script, and Otto said he would ask his mother about film-editing apps and all that. The others were supposed to think of some possible actors but not ask anybody until we knew what we needed.

Walking home my mind was racing. This was going to be so dope!

44

But it turned out to be worse than writing a paper for school! After dinner I sat at my desk for hours staring at the computer. Then I watched some more old horror movie clips to get ideas. Then Mom popped in and told me to go to bed. Then I couldn't sleep. So, I took my laptop and made a tent under the covers and tried to come up with an outline at least:

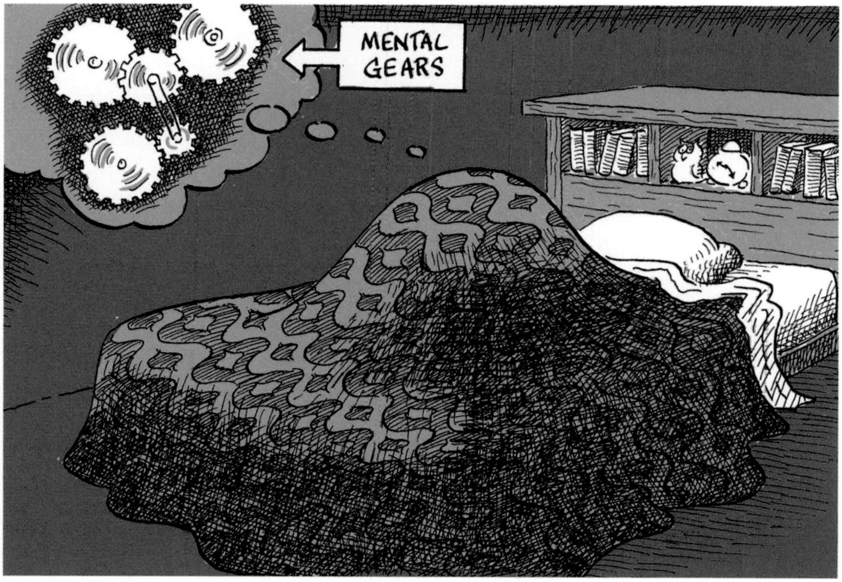
MENTAL GEARS

Scene 1 — Pretty girl walking through woods …

No, that was just like *Creatures of the Night*.

DELETE!

Scene 1 — Kids on beach having fun, eerie music, everyone stops and looks toward the ocean …

DELETE! DELETE! DELETE!

I was so tired I felt like crying. My eyes felt gritty.

"Anne?" It was Mom. I snapped my laptop shut.

"What are you doing under there? Is everything all right?"

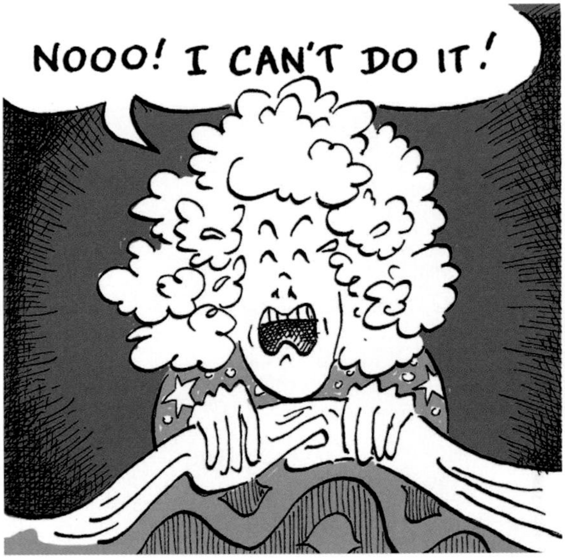
NOOO! I CAN'T DO IT!

Mom sat on the bed and put her arms around me. "Tell me about it," she said.

"I acted like a big shot!" I wailed. "I said I would be the director and I would write the script and I can't think of ANYTHING!"

"You're very tired, Anne," she said. "Why don't you lie down and ..."

"I can't sleep! I can't stop thinking about it — the same stupid things over and over and over ..."

"Okay," said Mom. "Tell me. You and your friends want to make a movie. A horror movie, you said?"

"We have a title," I said. "*Dracula Marries Frankenstein*. We want it to end with a wedding. But I don't know how it should start. Everything I think of is so ordinary and boring or comes from some other movie."

Mom smiled. "I like your title. It's funny. But the ending won't be a surprise if it's in the title. Maybe you should start with the wedding. That's different. Then you could make your movie about what happens after they get married. Maybe Frankenstein gets mad because Dracula sleeps all day."

"Yeah," I said, "And he doesn't help with the housework!"

Mom laughed. "I think they would be a very ill-suited couple. What happens when they go out to dinner together? Is Dracula tempted to bite Frankenstein on the neck?"

We were both laughing by then. And suddenly I couldn't keep my eyes open.

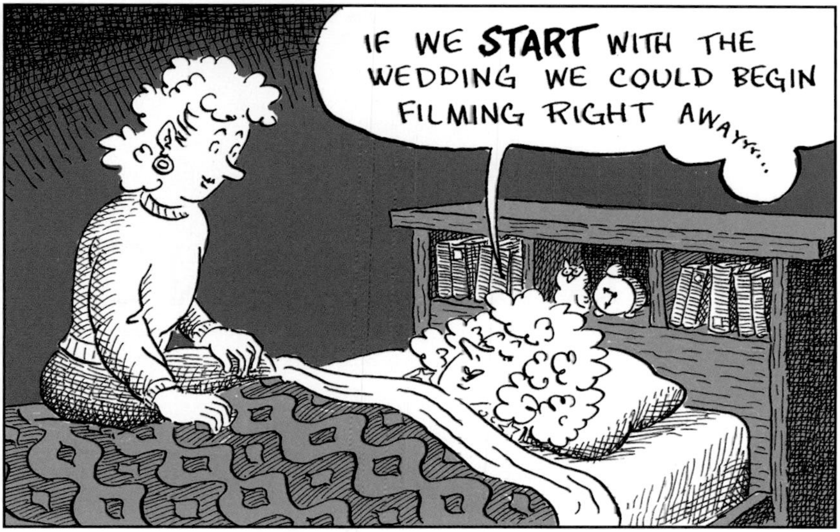
IF WE **START** WITH THE WEDDING WE COULD BEGIN FILMING RIGHT AWAYYY...

7

THE WEDDING

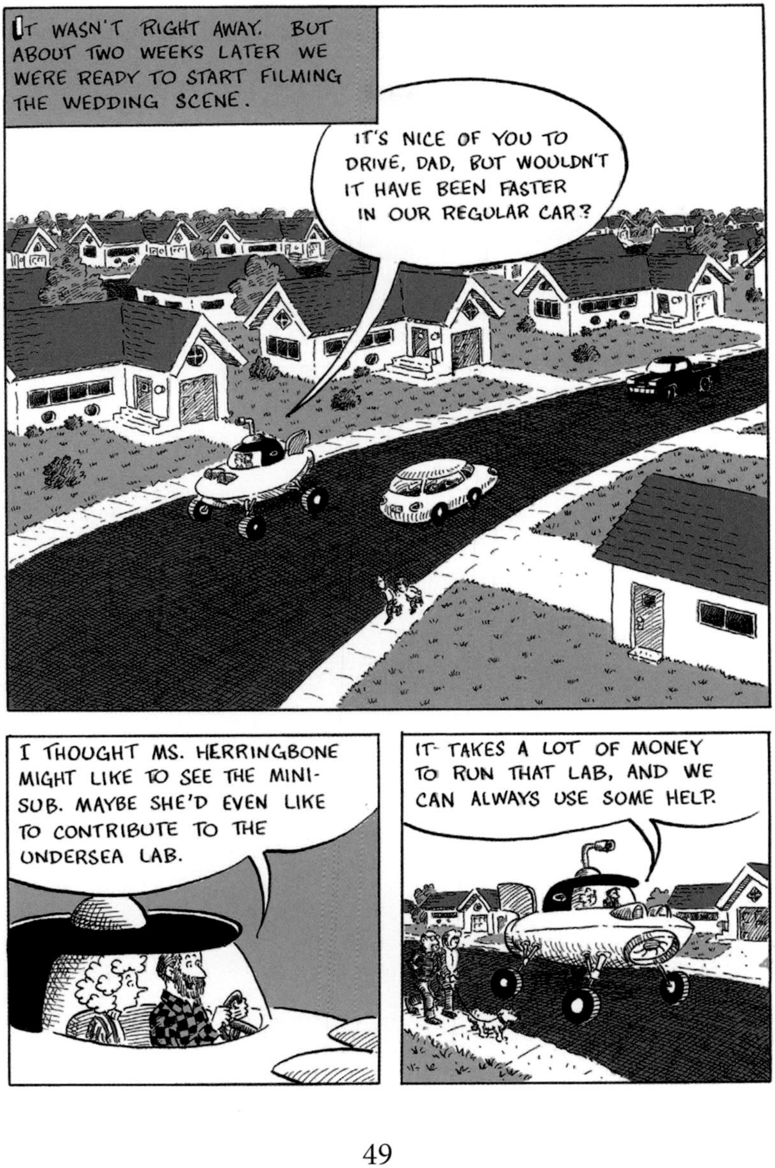
IT WASN'T RIGHT AWAY. BUT ABOUT TWO WEEKS LATER WE WERE READY TO START FILMING THE WEDDING SCENE.
IT'S NICE OF YOU TO DRIVE, DAD, BUT WOULDN'T IT HAVE BEEN FASTER IN OUR REGULAR CAR?
I THOUGHT MS. HERRINGBONE MIGHT LIKE TO SEE THE MINI-SUB. MAYBE SHE'D EVEN LIKE TO CONTRIBUTE TO THE UNDERSEA LAB.
IT TAKES A LOT OF MONEY TO RUN THAT LAB, AND WE CAN ALWAYS USE SOME HELP.

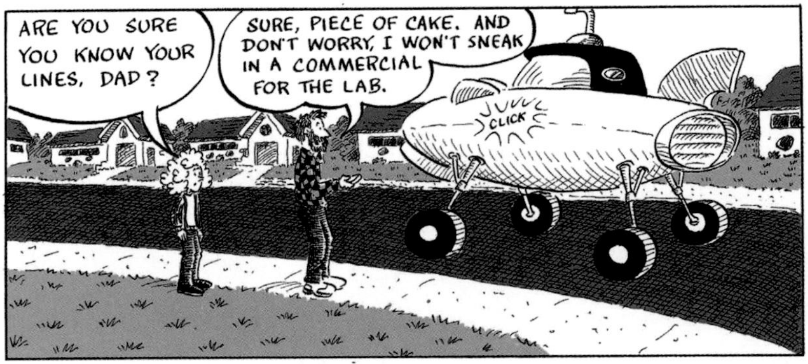

ARE YOU SURE YOU KNOW YOUR LINES, DAD?
SURE, PIECE OF CAKE. AND DON'T WORRY, I WON'T SNEAK IN A COMMERCIAL FOR THE LAB.
CLICK

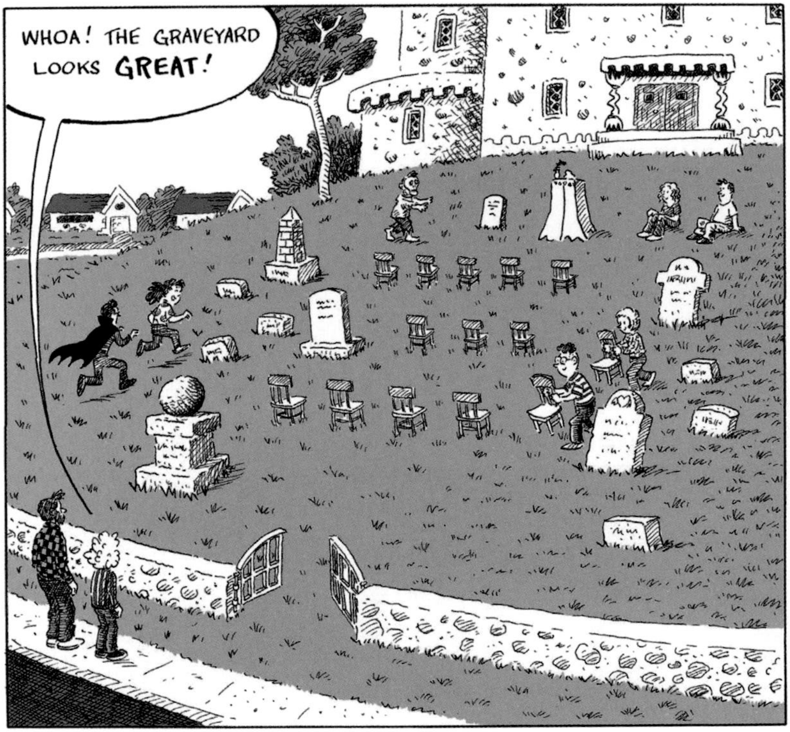

WHOA! THE GRAVEYARD LOOKS **GREAT**!

THEY'RE GETTING MARRIED IN A GRAVEYARD?
ISN'T IT PERFECT? ALL OF MS. HERRING-BONE'S ANCESTORS ARE BURIED IN HER BACKYARD!
WHAT'S WRONG WITH THOSE KIDS OVER THERE?
HAHA HA!
THEY'RE ALL SUPPOSED TO BE ZOMBIES AND MUMMIES AND STUFF.
NEED MEAT...
NEED BRAINS...
EBENEZER HERRINGBONE 1820-1844

POPPY, I CAN HARDLY BELIEVE IT! THE COSTUMES LOOK AWESOME!
THANKS, ANNE.
WHAT'S THAT ON YOUR PHONE?
IT'S A CLIP-ON LENS THAT SHOULD GIVE US SHARPER PICTURES.
ANNE, WHICH ONE IS MS. HERRINGBONE?
SHE'S NOT ONE OF THE ZOMBIES, DAD.
THERE SHE IS! C'MON, I'LL INTRODUCE YOU.
Mr. Blossom, I must congratulate you on your charming and clever offspring!

OKAY, FIRST LET'S GET SOME SHOTS OF THE GUESTS COMING INTO THE GRAVEYARD AND TAKING THEIR SEATS.

GET PLENTY OF FOOTAGE. WE CAN EDIT IT LATER.

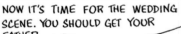
NOW IT'S TIME FOR THE WEDDING SCENE. YOU SHOULD GET YOUR FATHER.

WE'RE FINALLY MAKING OUR MOVIE. ISN'T THIS EXCITING?

OKAY, NOW MR. ROCK PLAYS THE MINISTER FOR THE WEDDING. YOU'RE JUST THE VOICE OF MR. ROCK, SO WE DON'T WANT TO SEE YOU. JUST STAY COVERED AND BEGIN YOUR LINES AFTER THE MUSIC STOPS.

MUSIC'S GOOD TO GO. ARE YOU READY, BRENDAN?
SHOULDN'T FRANKENSTEIN BE HERE BY NOW? WHO DID YOU GET TO PLAY HIM, ANYWAY?
SEE FOR YOURSELF. HERE HE COMES NOW!
IT'S GREGORY, MS. HERRINGBONE'S BUTLER!
OKAY, PLACES EVERYONE! OTTO, START THE MUSIC!

WEIRDLY BELOVED, WE ARE GATHERED HERE IN THIS APPROPRIATELY CREEPY GRAVEYARD FOR A MOST SOLEMN PURPOSE.
IT IS TO CELEBRATE THE MARRIAGE OF THIS VAMPIRE TO THIS MONSTER.
DRACULA, DO YOU PROMISE NEVER TO DRINK FRANKENSTEIN'S BLOOD WITHOUT SAYING PLEASE?
I DO.
AND FRANKENSTEIN --

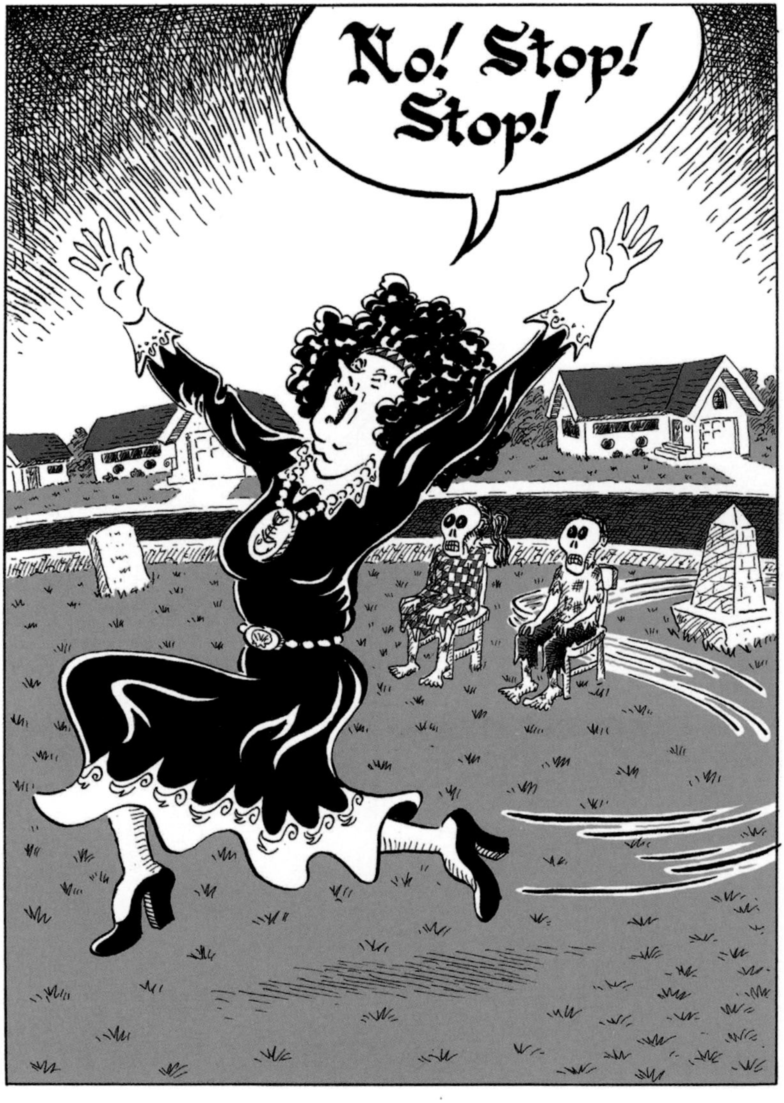
No! Stop! Stop!

What's going on here? Is this one of those Gay Marriages I've heard about?
Well, I won't have it! For 300 years my ancestors have rested peacefully in this graveyard. I cannot have them exposed to such repellent behavior!
HEY, IS THE SCENE FINISHED?
You!
Come along, Mr. Rock. I don't want you mixed up in this!
And Mr. Blossom, I am very disappointed in the way you are bringing up your daughter!

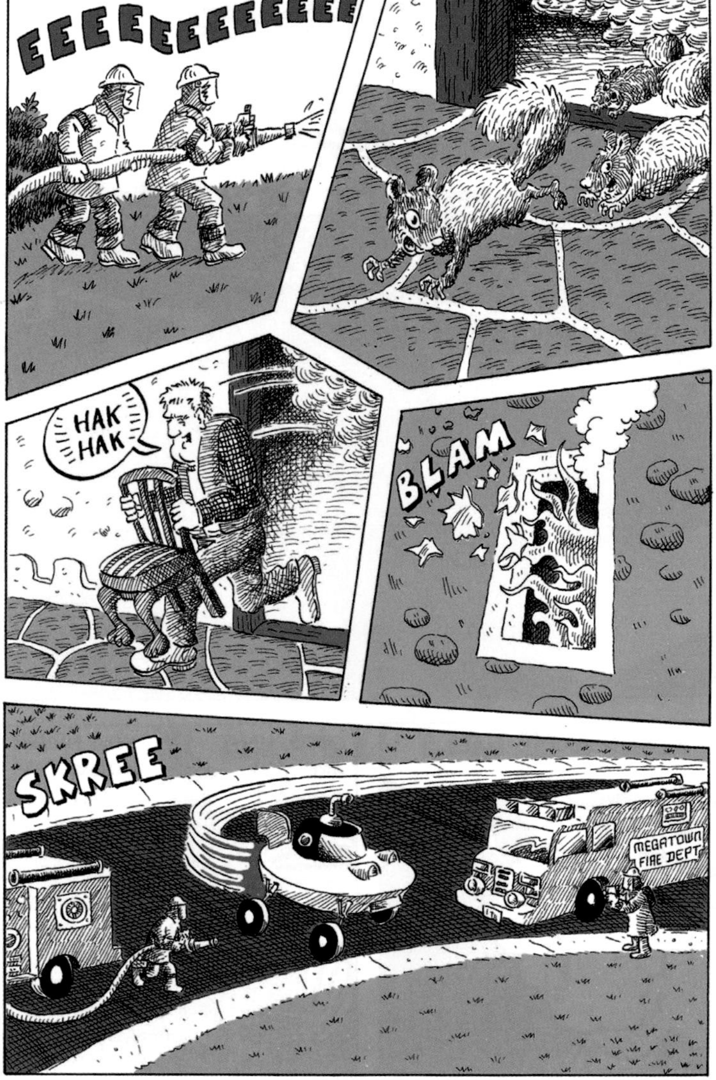
EEEEEEEEEEEE
HAK HAK
BLAM
SKREE
MEGATOWN FIRE DEPT

ANNE, WHEN DID THIS START?
I DON'T KNOW, DAD. WE JUST GOT HERE.
ANNE, LOOK!
OH, MY GOSH, IT'S MS. HERRINGBONE!
SHE'S TRAPPED!

WHAT'S SHE DOING?
THE LADDER TRUCK ISN'T HERE YET, BUT I CAN USE THE MINI-SUB.
MY DAD LOVES ANY OPPORTUNITY TO USE HIS MINI-SUB.
THERE GOES THE ROOF.
BEEP BEEP

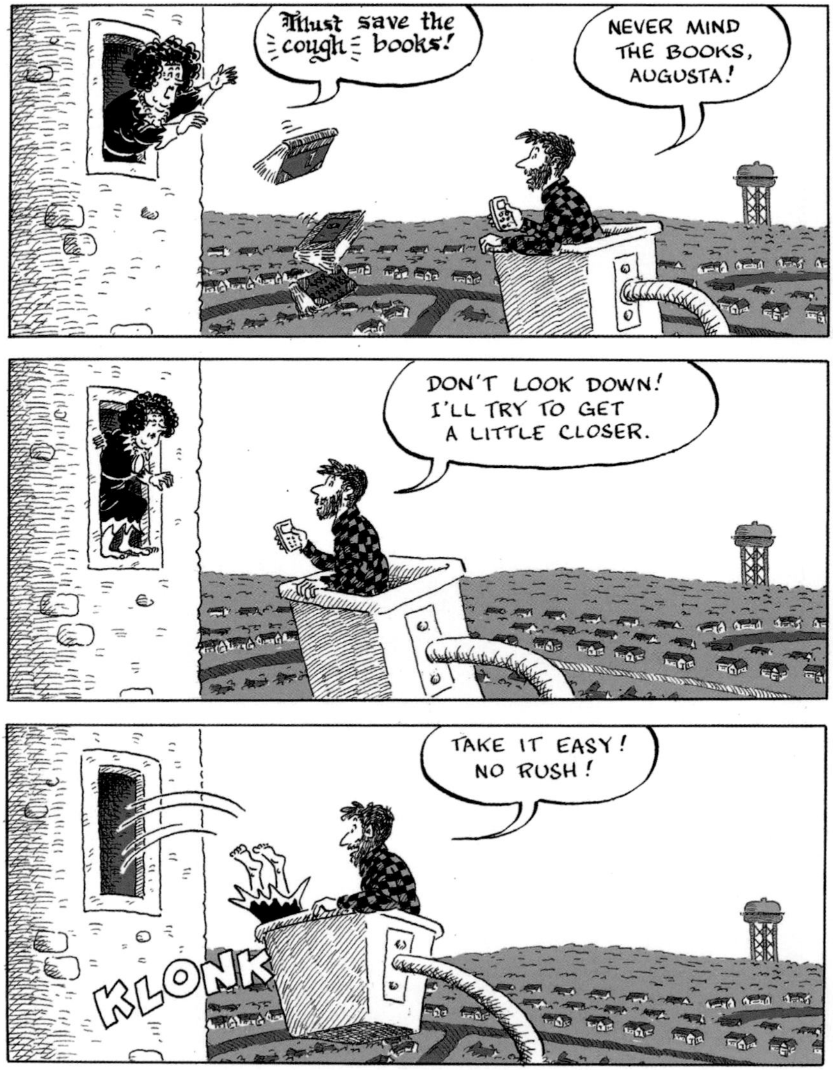
Must save the cough books!
NEVER MIND THE BOOKS, AUGUSTA!
DON'T LOOK DOWN! I'LL TRY TO GET A LITTLE CLOSER.
TAKE IT EASY! NO RUSH!
KLONK

HOW IS SHE?
I THINK SHE'S INHALED A LOT OF SMOKE.
YOU'LL BE FINE, AUGUSTA. I'M RIGHT HERE.
POOR MS. HERRINGBONE! SHE DIDN'T DESERVE THIS, EVEN IF SHE IS A LITTLE STRANGE.
MEGATOWN RESCUE
AMBULANCE

ALL RIGHT, FOLKS, THERE'S NOTHING MORE TO SEE.
DO YOU WANT A RIDE HOME, SWEETIE?
NO, THANKS, I'LL TAKE MY BIKE.
WELL, DON'T DAWDLE TOO LONG. IT LOOKS LIKE THERE'S A STORM COMING.

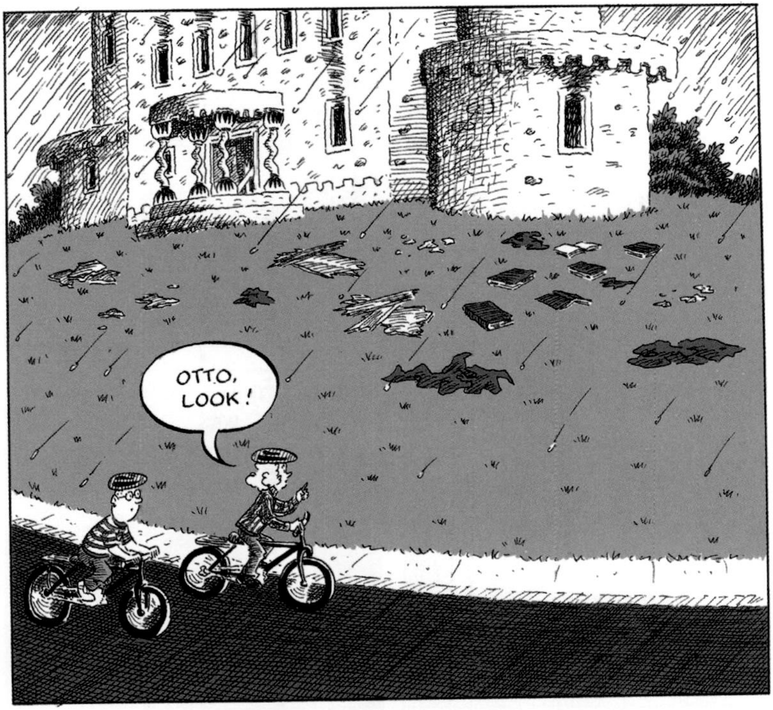
OTTO, LOOK!

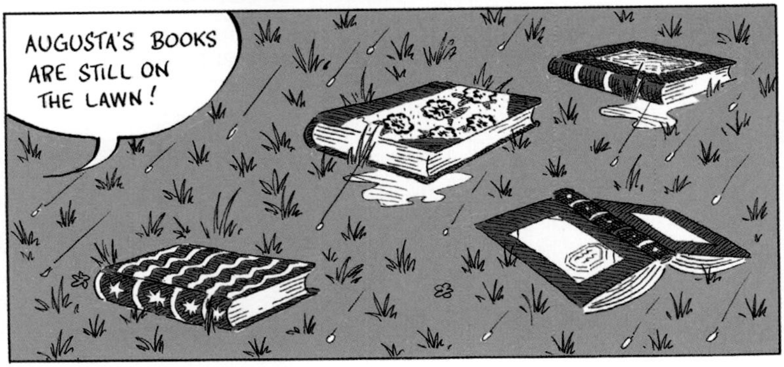
AUGUSTA'S BOOKS ARE STILL ON THE LAWN!

THESE ARE ALL OLD PHOTO ALBUMS.
LOOK AT THIS!
I'LL BET THAT'S MS. HERRINGBONE WHEN SHE WAS YOUNG.
KRAK
YOW! THAT WAS CLOSE! WE'D BETTER GET OUT OF HERE.

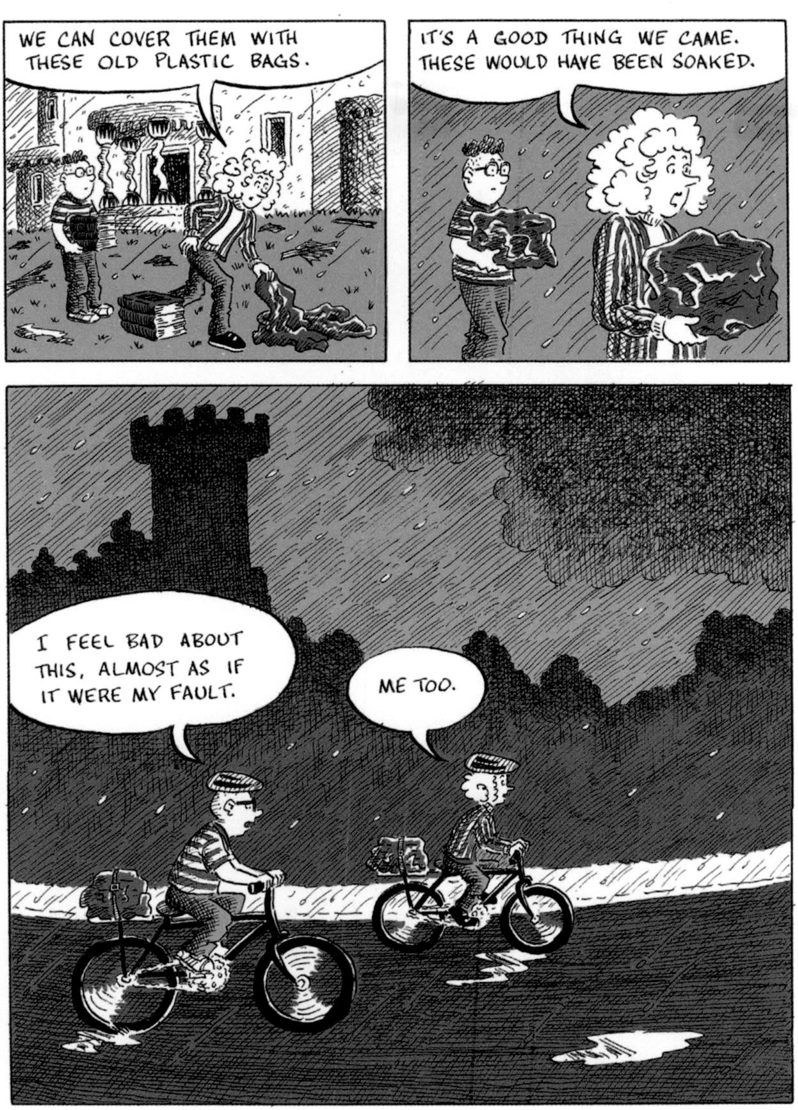
WE CAN COVER THEM WITH THESE OLD PLASTIC BAGS.
IT'S A GOOD THING WE CAME. THESE WOULD HAVE BEEN SOAKED.
I FEEL BAD ABOUT THIS, ALMOST AS IF IT WERE MY FAULT.
ME TOO.

10

ASHES

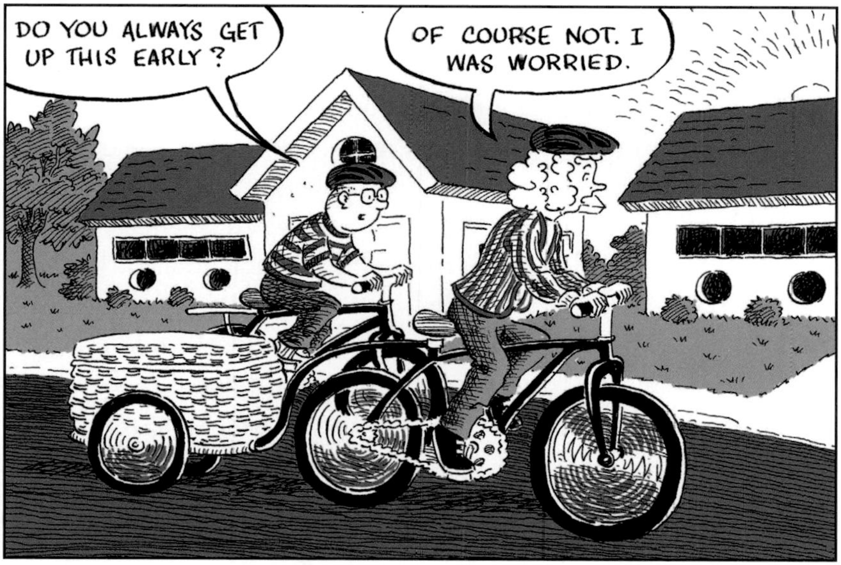
DO YOU ALWAYS GET UP THIS EARLY?
OF COURSE NOT. I WAS WORRIED.

We were pedaling back to the scene of the fire, and I had the trailer Dad had made for me hooked up to the back of my bike.

"Worried about what?" Otto asked, puffing along behind me.

"Tell you when we get there!" I called, freewheeling through the puddles on the Airport Road.

We stood our bikes by the curb. It was so early that no one else was around.

"You do realize, don't you," Otto said, "that this fire could have been set on purpose by one of those people who saw the video? We should be skipping town – not visiting the scene of the crime!"

"*That's* what I'm worried about. That somebody set the fire on purpose. Because of the video!"

"It's possible." Otto shrugged. "People do crazy things."

I ducked under the police tape.

"They put that there for a reason, you know," Otto said.

"I know, but I thought we should rescue Mr. Rock," I said. "And the other rocks too if we can."

"Why us?" Otto asked. "We aren't exactly Ms. Herringbone's nearest and dearest. Besides, everything is probably totaled. I bet they just bulldoze the whole place."

"Exactly! Who else is gonna save a few old rocks with faces?"

The front door was leaning half-open on one hinge. I pushed it wide and peaked in. The place stunk so bad of wet soot, it made my nose itch.

"I don't think this is a good idea." Otto hung back.

"I'm going in," I said.

Everything was black. I walked through the dark front hall trying to remember the way to the sitting room where we had met with Ms. Herringbone.

"Careful," said Otto, close behind me.

We tiptoed, testing each step, but the floor felt solid beneath our feet. There was a bright light at the end of the hall, and we gasped when we reached it.

The sitting room was completely open to the sky. The morning sun shone on jumbled piles of brick and boards, broken glass and shattered furniture, all black with soot and steaming gently as the morning sun warmed the stinky, waterlogged mess.

"We'll never find them," Otto whispered in my ear.

"I think they were over by this wall," I said, pushing a broken stool aside.

Soon we were as black and smelly as everything else. But we had assembled about fifteen dirty rocks on a dented tray, plus one that was almost too big to carry, but surprisingly light. I looked at them and frowned. Maybe this wasn't such a good idea after all.

Otto said, "We still haven't found Mr. Rock."

"How can you tell?" I asked him. "They all look the same to me."

"I don't know. None of these speak to me."

"Hah!" I said. "Maybe you should try calling him."

"Good idea," Otto said. And he actually went around the room, calling out to him.

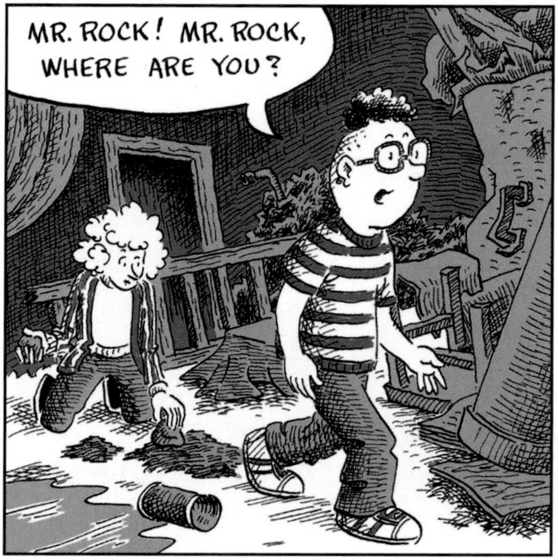
MR. ROCK! MR. ROCK, WHERE ARE YOU?

I said I thought we should leave before the police or somebody showed up, but Otto was busy poking around under some soggy cushions.

"Aha!" he said. "Gotcha." And there, clean from sheltering under his protective pillow, and smiling his usual calm smile, was Mr. Rock.

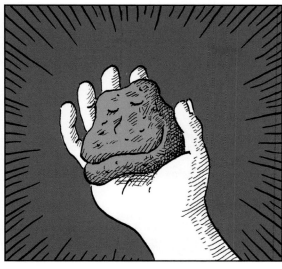

I didn't give Otto the satisfaction of asking him how he did that.

We left quickly, putting the rocks in the trailer.

"Now what?" said Otto.

"Now we take them to Ms. Herringbone," I said.

"What?!"

"In the hospital," I added.

"But she hates us!"

"I don't care. I need to explain. This video thing has been bothering me for weeks. And now the fire! She has to know that we didn't mean any harm. Besides, marriage between two men, or women for that matter, is legal!"

"You don't have to explain it to me," Otto said.

"So I'm hoping," I continued, "if we take her the albums we saved yesterday, and Mr. Rock and the others, she'll listen to us."

11

THE PARTY
VEGETABLES

THE NEXT DAY...

MEGATOWN HOSPITAL

KNOCK KNOCK

MS. HERRINGBONE, WE HOPE...
So nice to see you, dears! Come right in!
WE'RE SO SORRY THAT...
No need to fuss about it. I'm fine!
And what have we here? Bless you, sweet children! And Mr. Rock, I am so pleased that you seem to have survived the conflagration with minimal damage!
And my albums! How wonderful! I can't thank you enough!

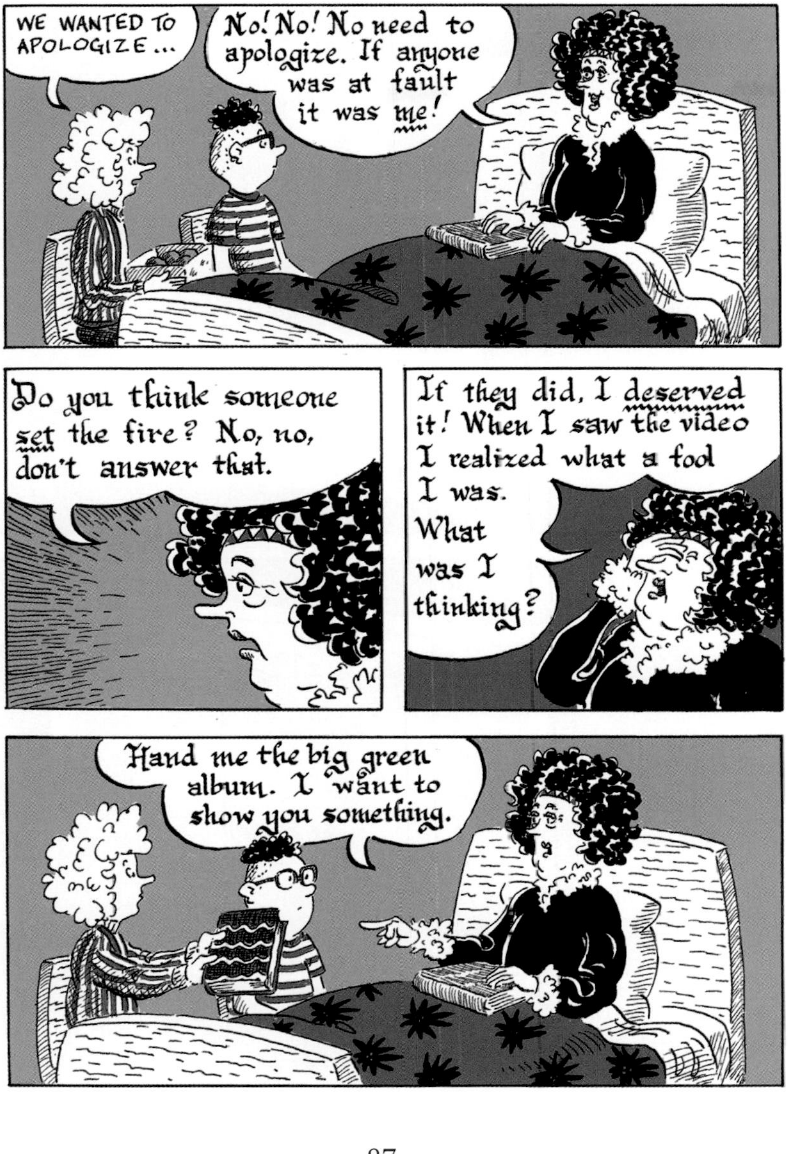
WE WANTED TO APOLOGIZE...
No! No! No need to apologize. If anyone was at fault it was me!
Do you think someone set the fire? No, no, don't answer that.
If they did, I deserved it! When I saw the video I realized what a fool I was.
What was I thinking?
Hand me the big green album. I want to show you something.

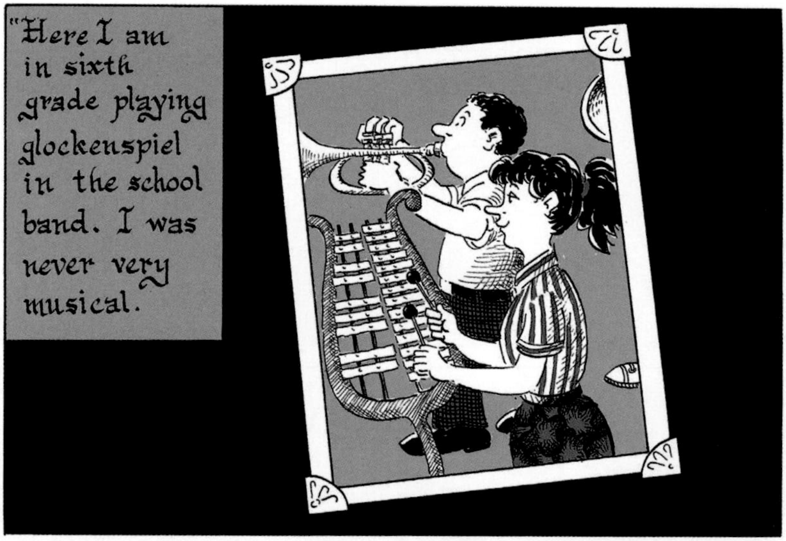
"Here I am in sixth grade playing glockenspiel in the school band. I was never very musical.

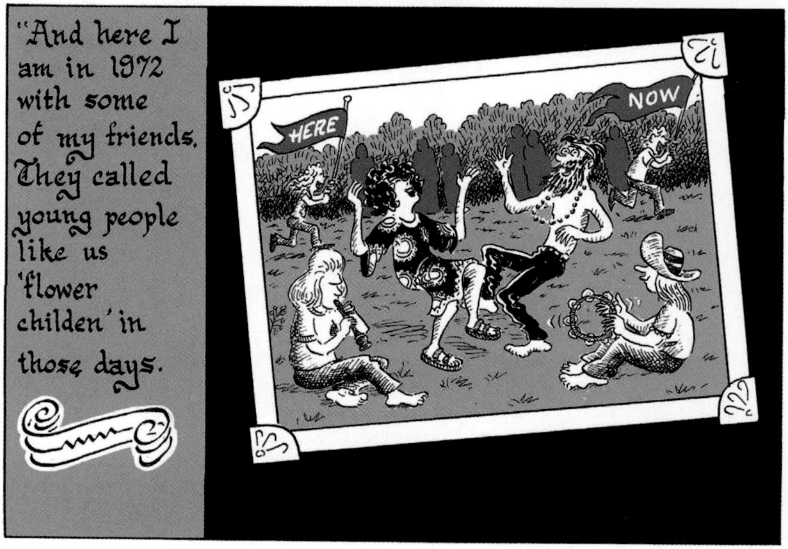
"And here I am in 1972 with some of my friends. They called young people like us 'flower children' in those days.
HERE
NOW

"Now this is what I wanted to show you. One summer we decided to make our own little home movie. We called it The Party Vegetables. Haha! Here I am trying on my costume for the first time."

This is our -- what do you call it? -- a mock-up for our movie. We took photos of ourselves in costume and my friend Dan made up silly rhymes to tell what was happening. You can read it for yourselves.

"Here's my friend Alice's little sister. We let her play Rose Marie because she was so small. Later on in life she became a well-known yoga instructor.

She is just a little pea. Her parents named her Rose Marie.

"Here I am in my opening scene. I got the part of Sue Ellen Bean because I have always been rather slender."

She has three friends— Sue Ellen Bean, and Betty Squash and Josephine.

The girls hang out with Dan Potato,
the Pepper Boys, and Scott Tomato.

They all agree it would be cool
to throw a party after school.

They tell their friends
to come at five.

They make the punch.
The guests arrive.

"Oh, no!" Rose cries.
"Here comes a worm!"

Scott tickles it
and makes it squirm.

Jo Beet is scared
and runs away.

Rose quickly tells
the band to play.

The worm stands up and starts to dance.
"Go, worm, go!" the singer chants.

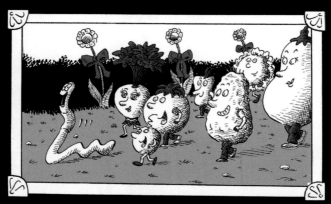

Their rules are few, but this one's firm --
To every party ask a worm!

THAT SOUNDS SO FUN! I **LOVE** IT. CAN WE SEE THE MOVIE?
I'm afraid it was never finished. You see, during the course of the filming Dan and I became more than just friends...
WERE YOU IN LOVE?
I thought we were. I was even planning our wedding.
And then something terrible happened...
Dan ran off with Scott Tomato!

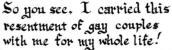

So you see, I carried this resentment of gay couples with me for my whole life!

I tried to deny how badly I was hurt, but when Dracula married Frankenstein it all seemed to come flooding back.

And now, goodness, how foolish I feel!

But don't worry about anything. The fire was probably caused by a faulty wire.

And once I get out of here we'll find a way to finish your movie, same-sex monster marriage and all.

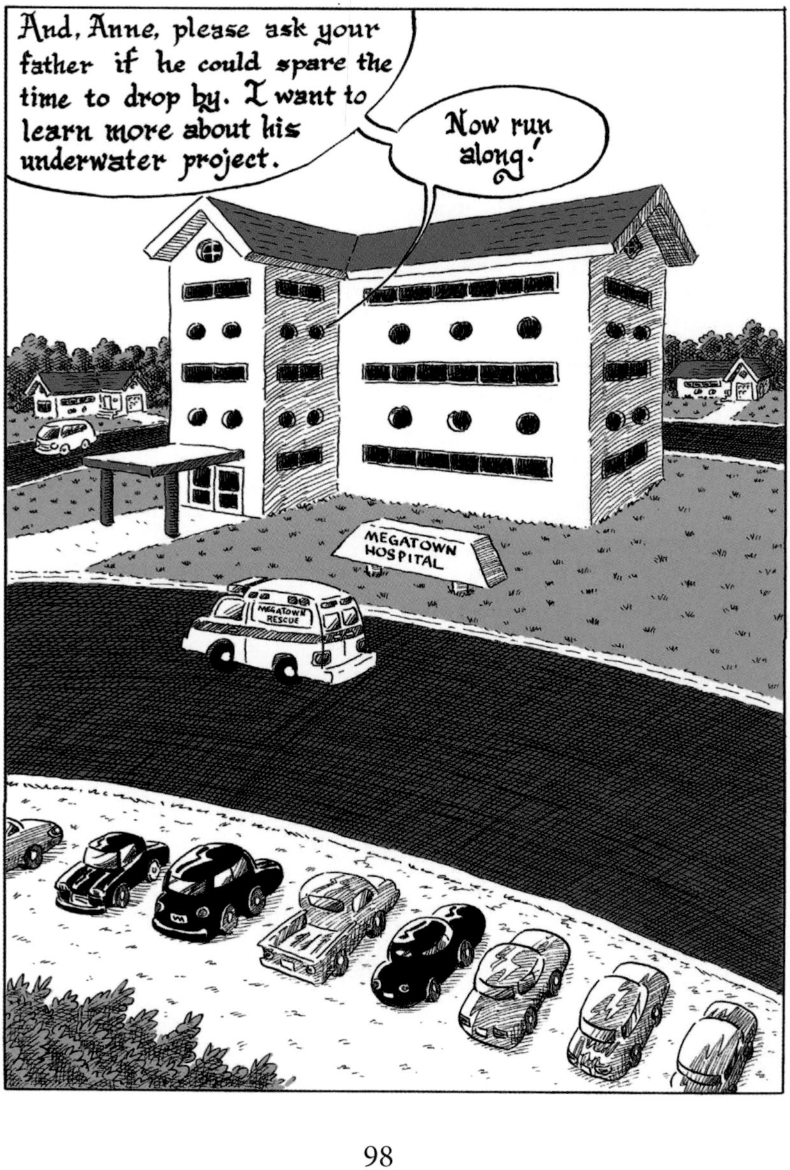
And, Anne, please ask your father if he could spare the time to drop by. I want to learn more about his underwater project.
Now run along!
MEGATOWN HOSPITAL
MEGATOWN RESCUE

12

AUGUSTA'S DECISION

After she got out of the hospital, Ms. Herringbone had to move, temporarily, into a Megatown house with Gregory. She said to Otto and me that, although it was smaller than she was used to, it wasn't as bad as she had expected. She also said with a happy smile, "Please call me Augusta. I feel like a girl again!"

I guess she decided that the Megatown house wasn't exactly her dream home, because Dad announced one evening, soon after that, that she was hiring him to build her an underwater dome.

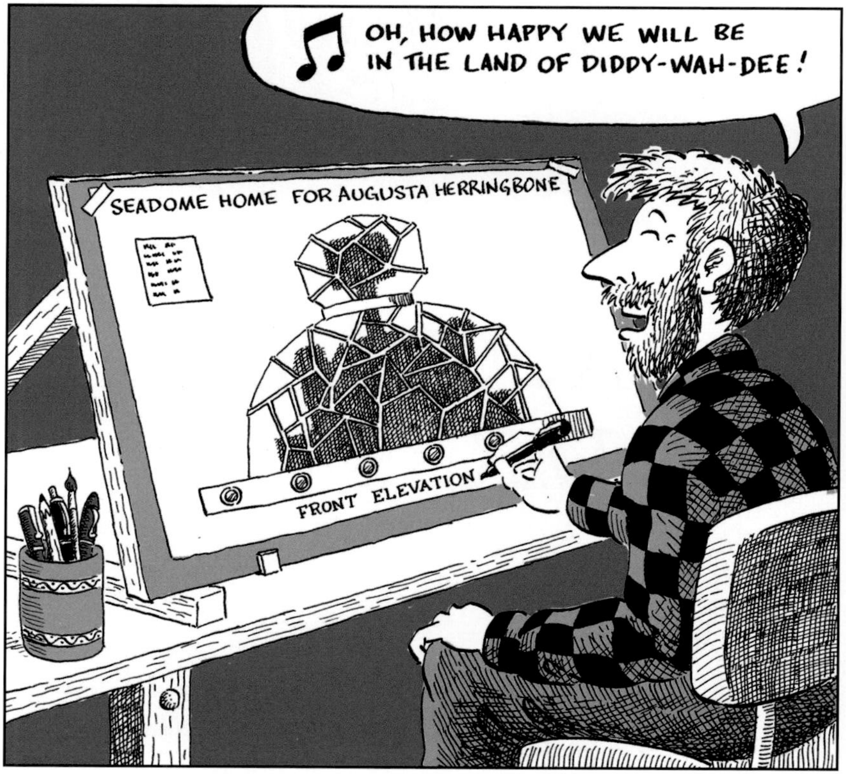
♫ OH, HOW HAPPY WE WILL BE IN THE LAND OF DIDDY-WAH-DEE!
SEADOME HOME FOR AUGUSTA HERRINGBONE
FRONT ELEVATION

It's been like heaven for him. He's been singing loud nonsense songs to himself over his drawing board, consulting with strange scientists, and phoning Augusta at all hours. They've been filming the building progress and Dad has given us lots of cool footage to use in our new video. They call the new house the Sea Dome.

Meanwhile, we got busy finishing our horror movie. Actually, it turned out to be more of a comedy than a horror movie, but I didn't mind. We had decided to splice in some of Otto's video of the fire as a dramatic ending to the wedding scene, so then Dracula and Frankenstein have to go live in an ordinary Megatown house (just like Augusta and Gregory), and that gave us some good ideas for funny scenes. They have no basements in Megatown, for example, so there's no good place for Dracula's coffin. And Frankenstein is always getting mad at Dracula for sleeping all day and not helping with the housework. And Dracula doesn't like to argue, so he turns into a bat and flies away, which really makes Frankenstein fume.

We kept cracking ourselves up during filming, so I think it will be pretty funny when Otto and his mom finish editing it. We hope it will be ready for a premiere showing at Augusta's housewarming party in the Sea Dome.

So, all in all, it's been a great summer.

We shot the last scene in our movie, where all the monsters in the neighborhood have a party on the beach. Aferwards Otto and Brendan were packing up our gear for the last time. And Gregory and I walked down to the breakwater and watched Dad's mini-sub drive into the waves. It disappeared with a sucking squelch of seawater.

"What do you think, Gregory?" I asked him. "Will Augusta be

happy living in the Sea Dome?"

Gregory grinned eerily through his Frankenstein make-up. "Never have I seen her so happy," he boomed with dramatic flair. "This devastation of her family home, this freedom from the burden of 'the legacy of the Herringbones,' this has been her salvation! She is a changed woman!"

Gregory is also a changed man, and I give myself some of the credit for that. He's planning to pursue a career in Hollywood, acting and voicing animated films. My dad is fixing him up with an old friend of his who's in the business.

We watched the sun set over the water, then Gregory gave some of us rides home in Augusta's Rolls Royce.

Summer was almost over.

13

THE
DOMEWARMING

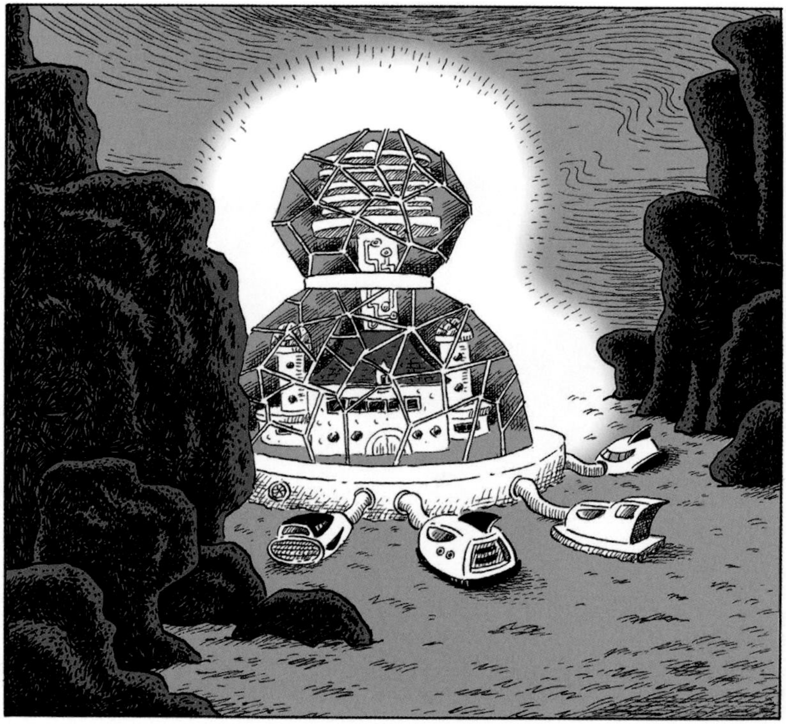

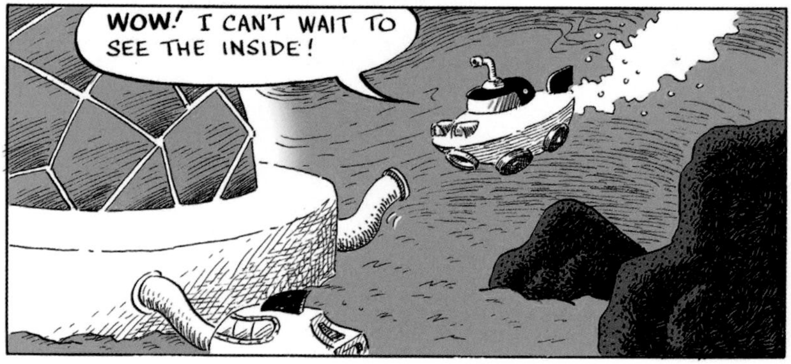
WOW! I CAN'T WAIT TO SEE THE INSIDE!

Welcome, welcome! I'm so glad you all could come!
I'd like you to meet my very special friends– Dan and Scott!
DAN, YOU WERE SO SPECIAL AS DAN POTATO!
OH, PLEASE! I WAS COMPLETELY OVERSHADOWED BY SCOTT'S PORTRAYAL OF SCOTT TOMATO!
You were both wonderful! And now I'd like you to meet Brendan, who plays Dracula in the movie.
'SUP?

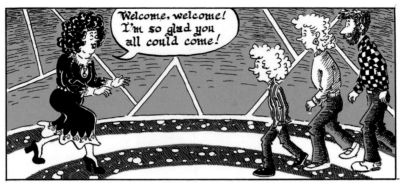

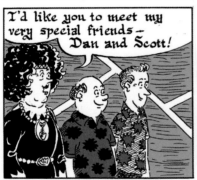

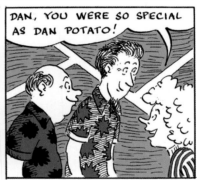

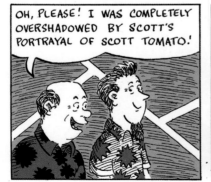

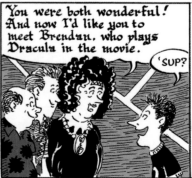

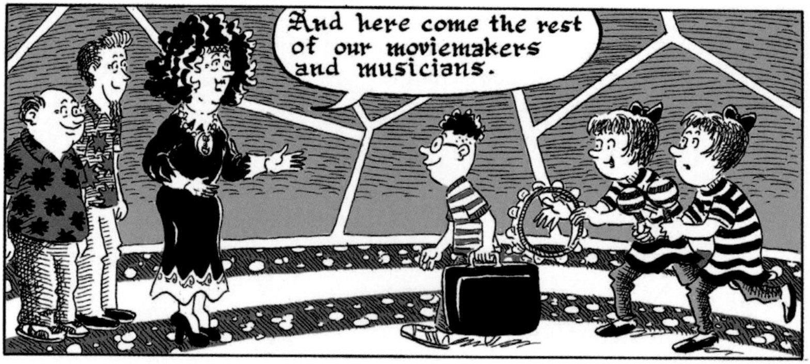
And here come the rest of our moviemakers and musicians.

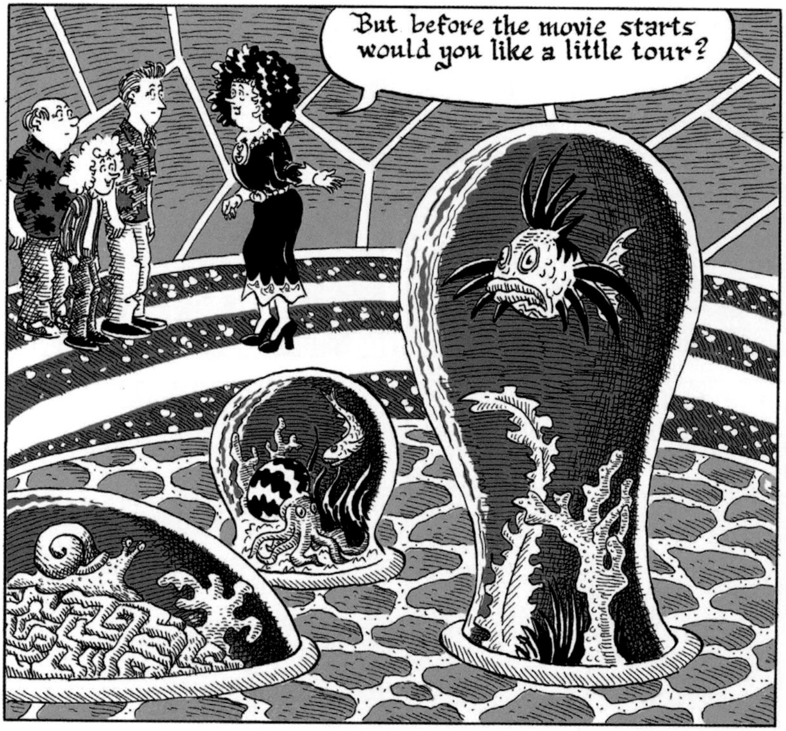
But before the movie starts would you like a little tour?

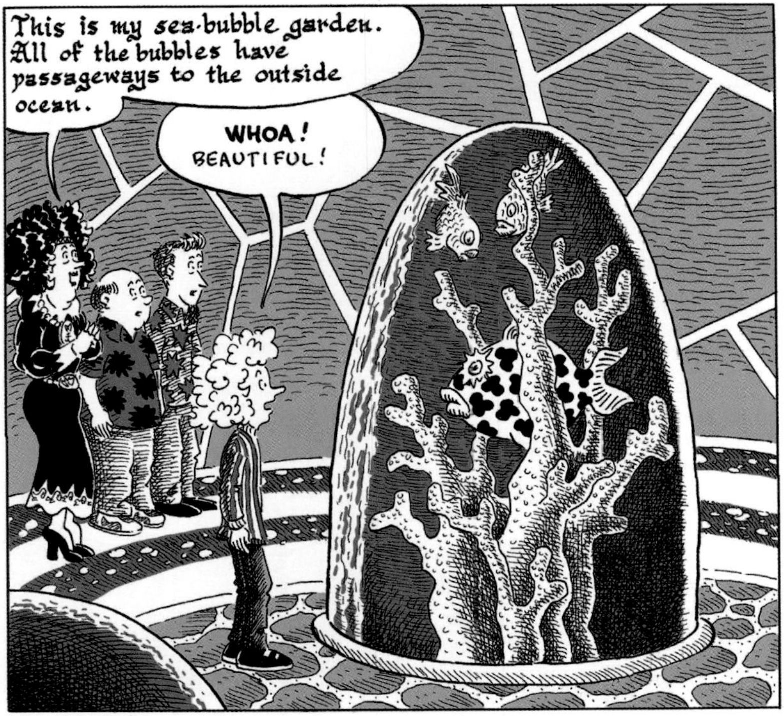
This is my sea-bubble garden. All of the bubbles have passageways to the outside ocean.
WHOA! BEAUTIFUL!

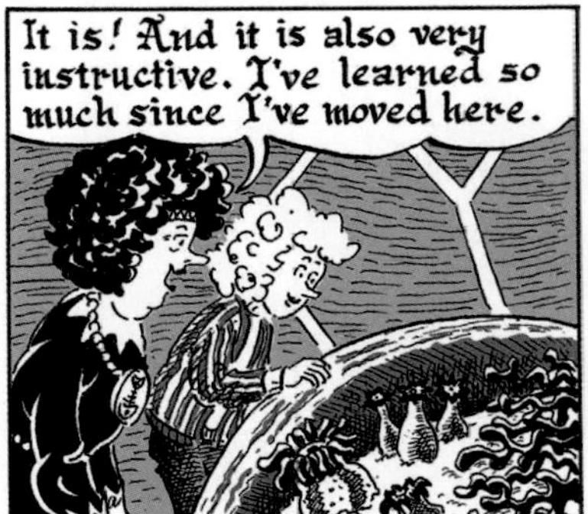
It is! And it is also very instructive. I've learned so much since I've moved here.

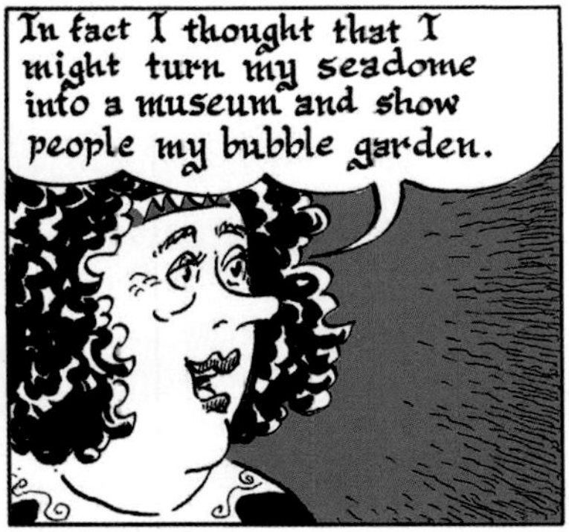
In fact I thought that I might turn my seadome into a museum and show people my bubble garden.

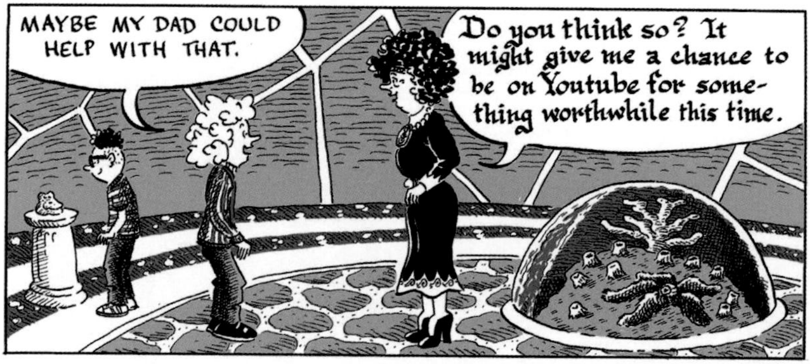
MAYBE MY DAD COULD HELP WITH THAT.
Do you think so? It might give me a chance to be on Youtube for something worthwhile this time.

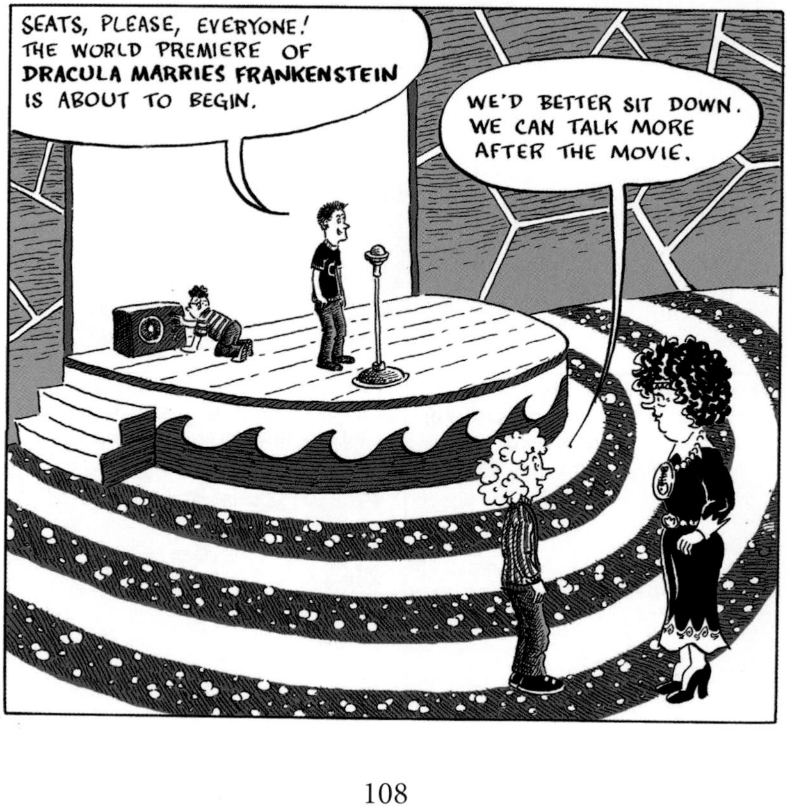
SEATS, PLEASE, EVERYONE! THE WORLD PREMIERE OF DRACULA MARRIES FRANKENSTEIN IS ABOUT TO BEGIN.
WE'D BETTER SIT DOWN. WE CAN TALK MORE AFTER THE MOVIE.

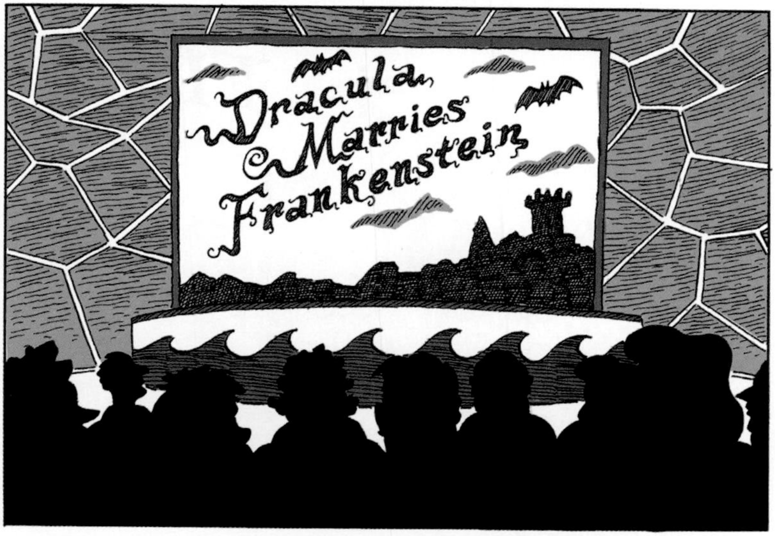
Dracula Marries Frankenstein

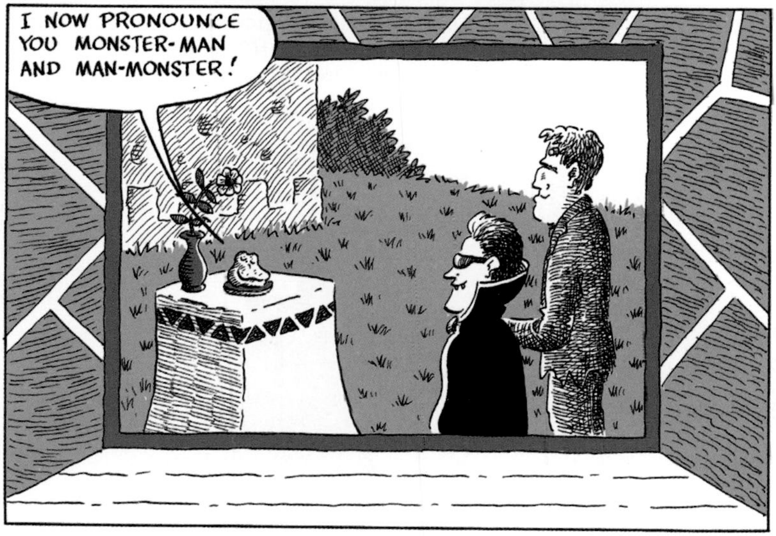
I NOW PRONOUNCE YOU MONSTER-MAN AND MAN-MONSTER!

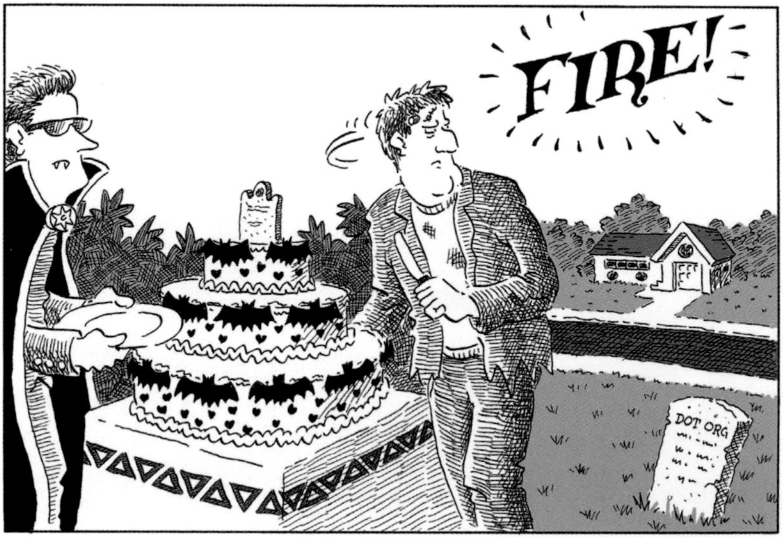
FIRE!
DOT ORG

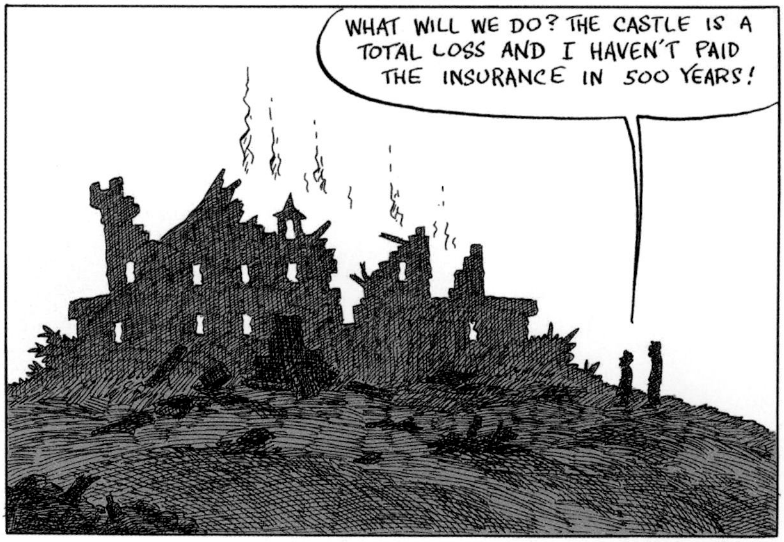
WHAT WILL WE DO? THE CASTLE IS A TOTAL LOSS AND I HAVEN'T PAID THE INSURANCE IN 500 YEARS!

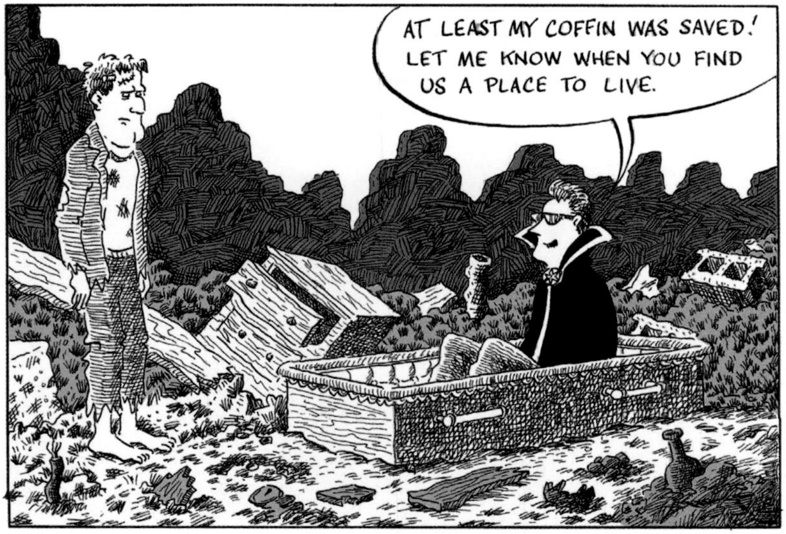
AT LEAST MY COFFIN WAS SAVED! LET ME KNOW WHEN YOU FIND US A PLACE TO LIVE.

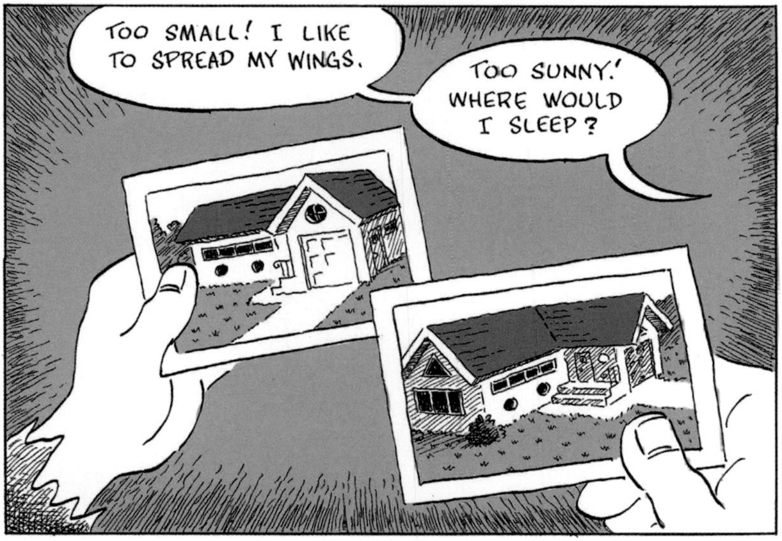
TOO SMALL! I LIKE TO SPREAD MY WINGS.
TOO SUNNY! WHERE WOULD I SLEEP?

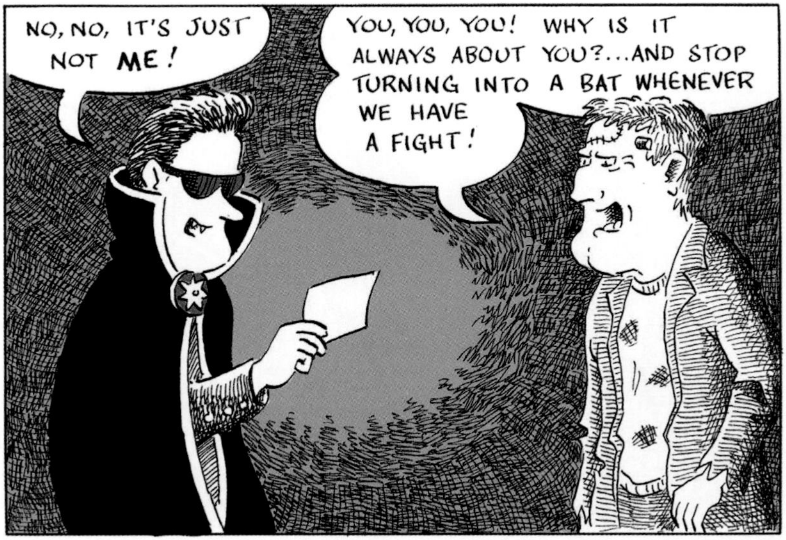
NO, NO, IT'S JUST NOT ME!
YOU, YOU, YOU! WHY IS IT ALWAYS ABOUT YOU?...AND STOP TURNING INTO A BAT WHENEVER WE HAVE A FIGHT!

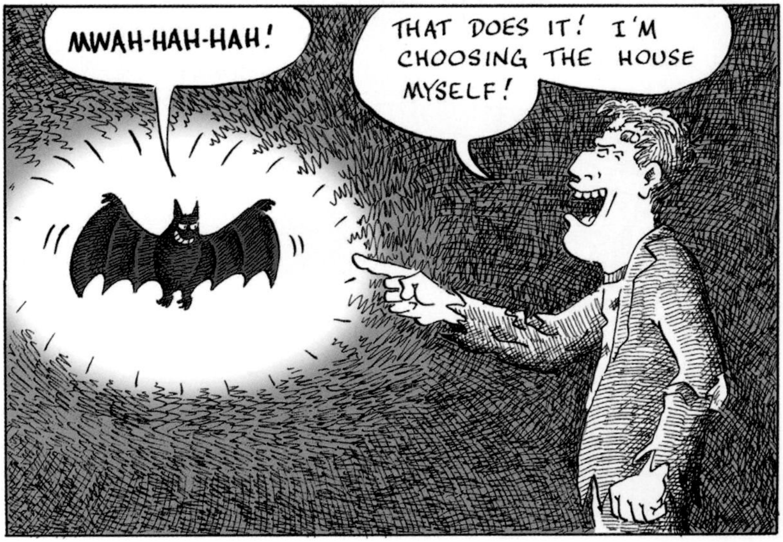
MWAH-HAH-HAH!
THAT DOES IT! I'M CHOOSING THE HOUSE MYSELF!

I LIKE LIVING HERE. THESE LITTLE MEGATOWN HOUSES HAVE ALL THE LATEST CONVENIENCES.
WHIRRR
I KNOW. ALL WE NEEDED WERE A FEW COBWEBS AND SOME HEAVY CURTAINS.
IT'S BEEN SO WARM TODAY, I THOUGHT WE COULD JUST HAVE BLOOD SHAKES FOR DINNER.
MMMM. I LOVE THE EYEBALL GARNISH!

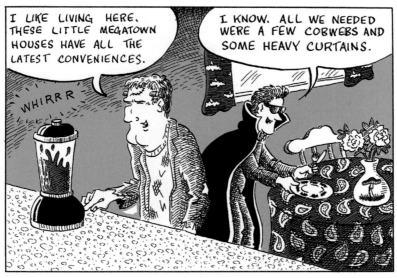

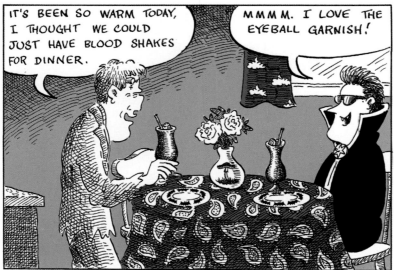

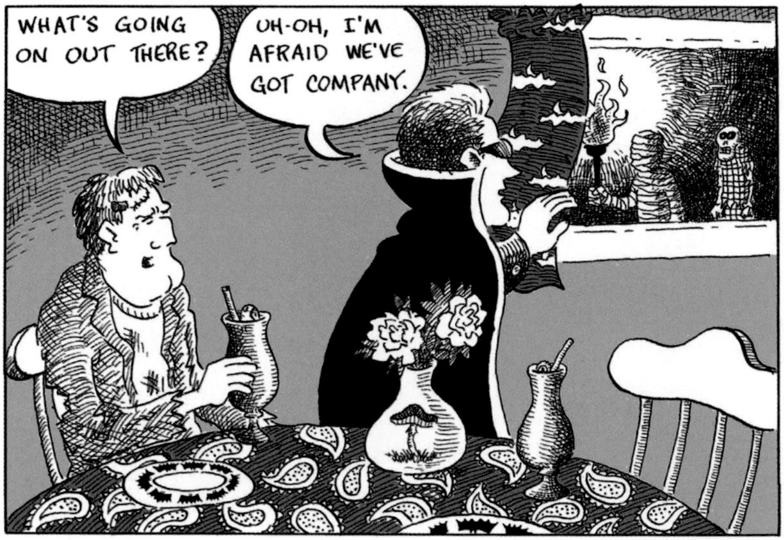
WHAT'S GOING ON OUT THERE?
UH-OH, I'M AFRAID WE'VE GOT COMPANY.

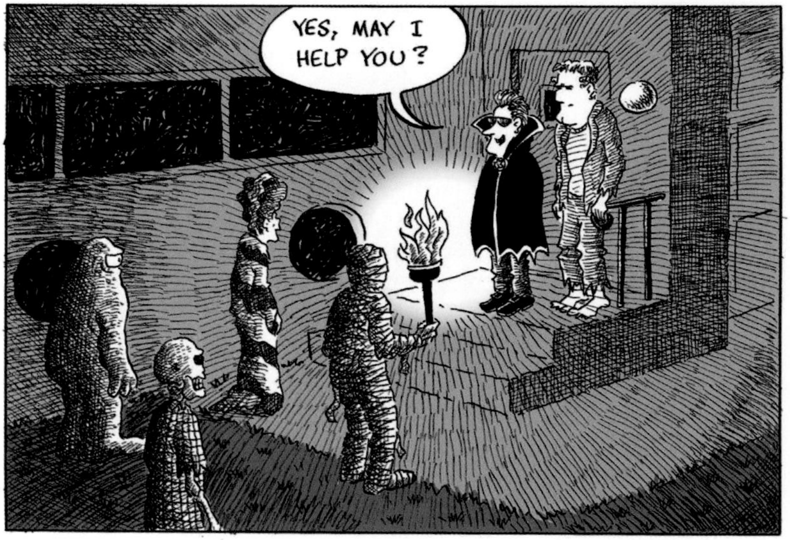
YES, MAY I HELP YOU?

SORRY TO BARGE IN LIKE THIS, BUT WE HEARD SOME NEW MONSTERS HAD MOVED IN ON MISTLETOE LANE, AND WE THOUGHT YOU MIGHT LIKE TO MEET SOME OF YOUR NEIGHBORS.
ABSOLUTELY!
The End
CLAP CLAP
CLAP CLAP

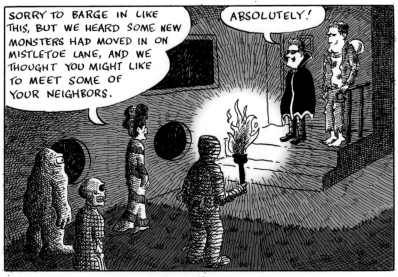

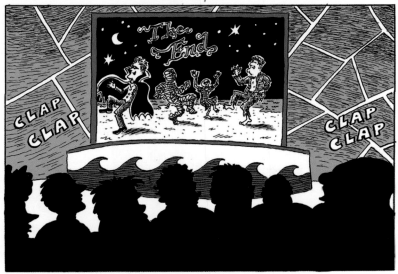

THANKS FOR WATCHING OUR MOVIE! AS SOME OF YOU MAY KNOW, WE'RE ALREADY PLANNING OUR NEXT FILM: **INVASION OF THE SLIMY SPONGE PEOPLE!** AND ONCE AGAIN AUGUSTA IS LETTING US USE HER HOME.

WE ALREADY HAVE OUR THEME SONG FOR IT. IT'S CALLED **DOWNSIDE UP** AND WE'D LIKE TO PLAY IT FOR YOU NOW! SPECIAL EFFECTS THANKS TO OTTO'S MOM!

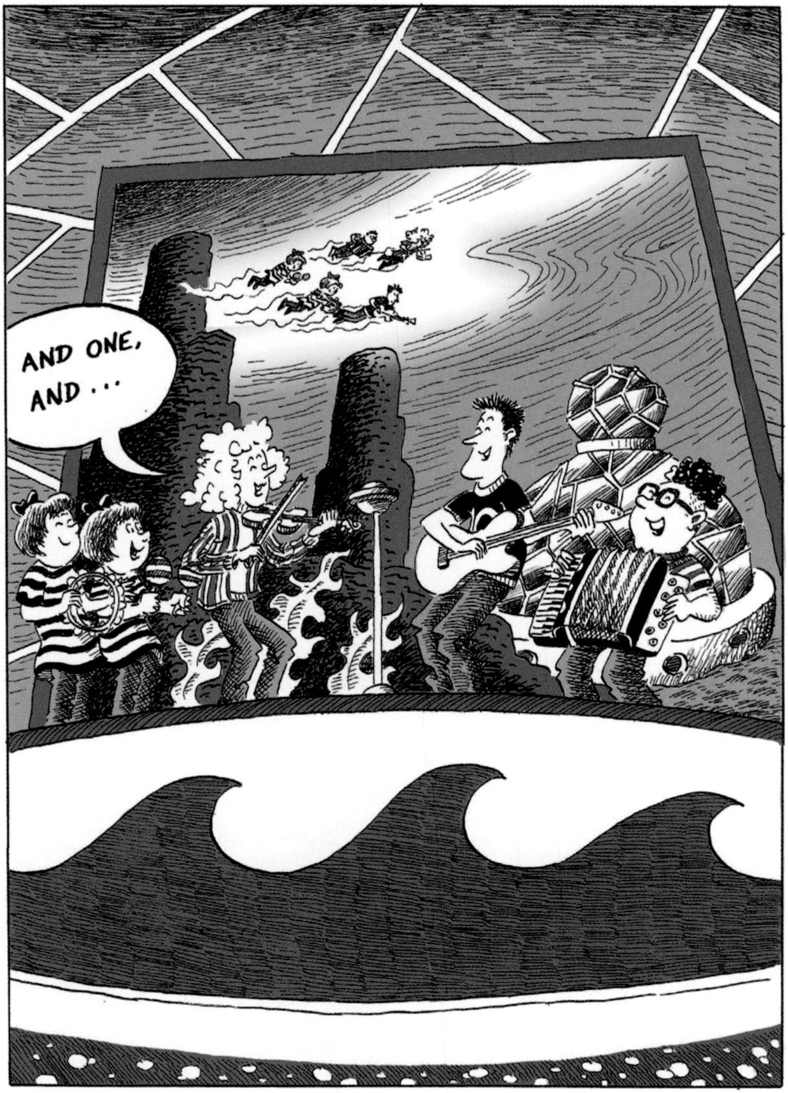
AND ONE, AND . . .

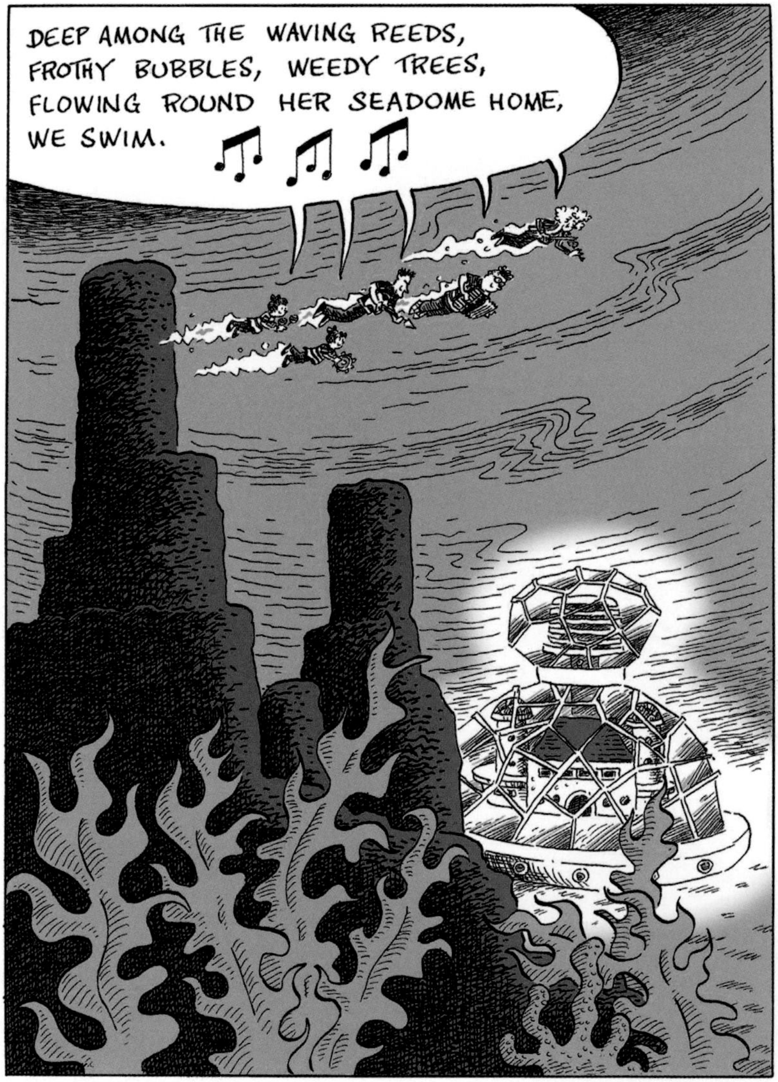
DEEP AMONG THE WAVING REEDS,
FROTHY BUBBLES, WEEDY TREES,
FLOWING ROUND HER SEADOME HOME,
WE SWIM.

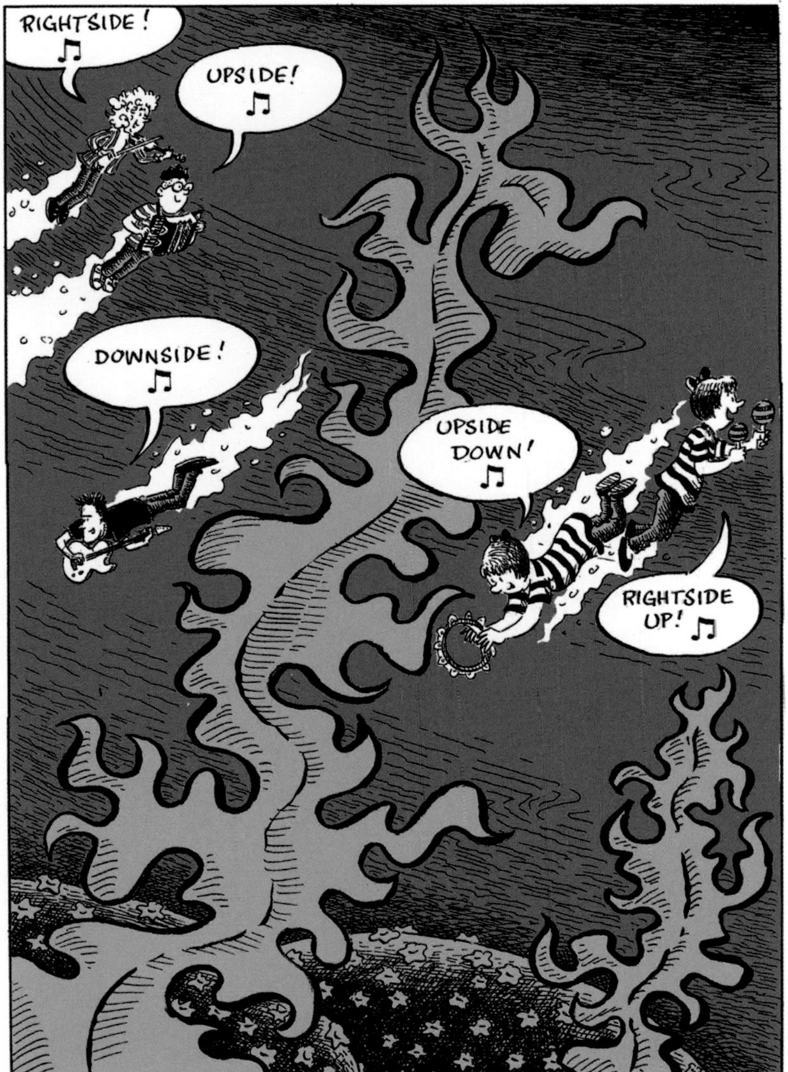
RIGHTSIDE! ♫
UPSIDE! ♫
DOWNSIDE! ♫
UPSIDE DOWN! ♫
RIGHTSIDE UP! ♫

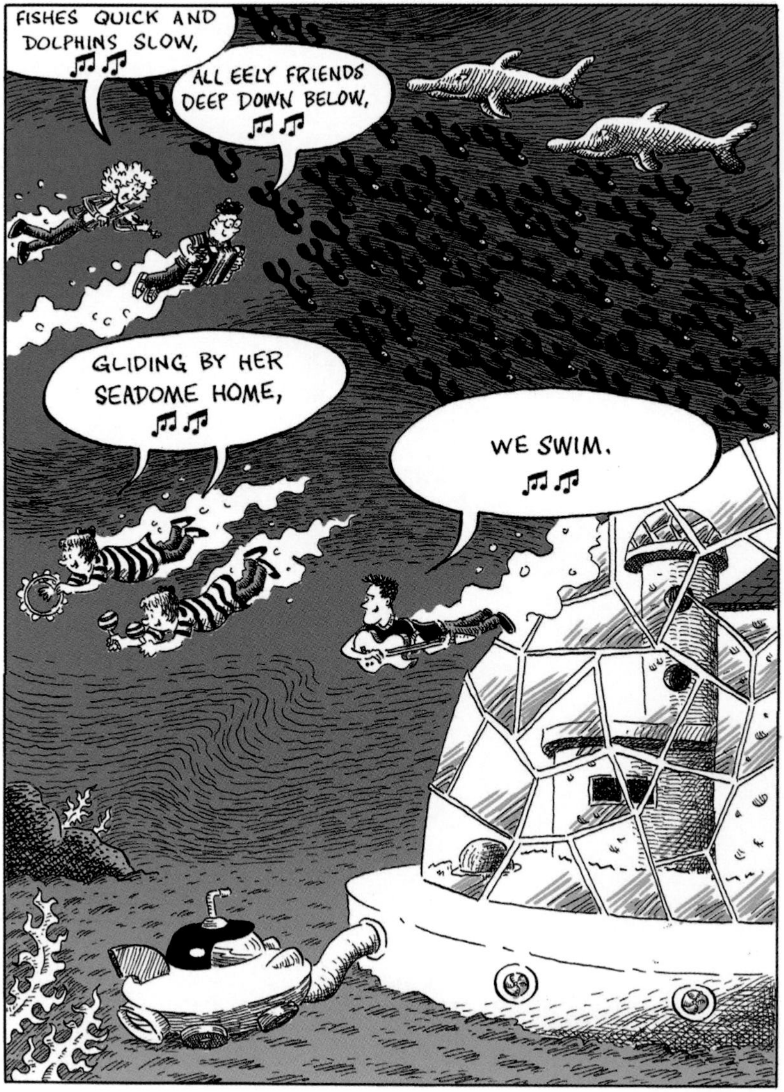
FISHES QUICK AND DOLPHINS SLOW, ♫♫
ALL EELY FRIENDS DEEP DOWN BELOW, ♫♫
GLIDING BY HER SEADOME HOME, ♫♫
WE SWIM. ♫♫

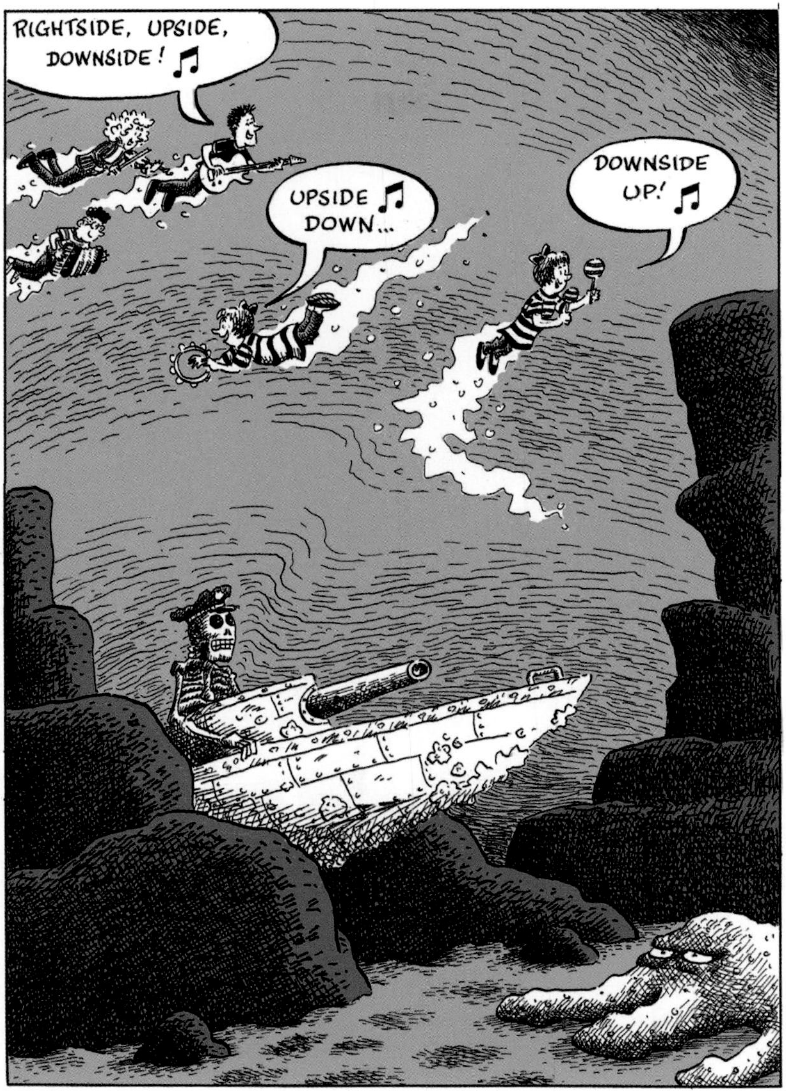
RIGHTSIDE, UPSIDE, DOWNSIDE! ♫
UPSIDE ♫ DOWN...
DOWNSIDE UP! ♫

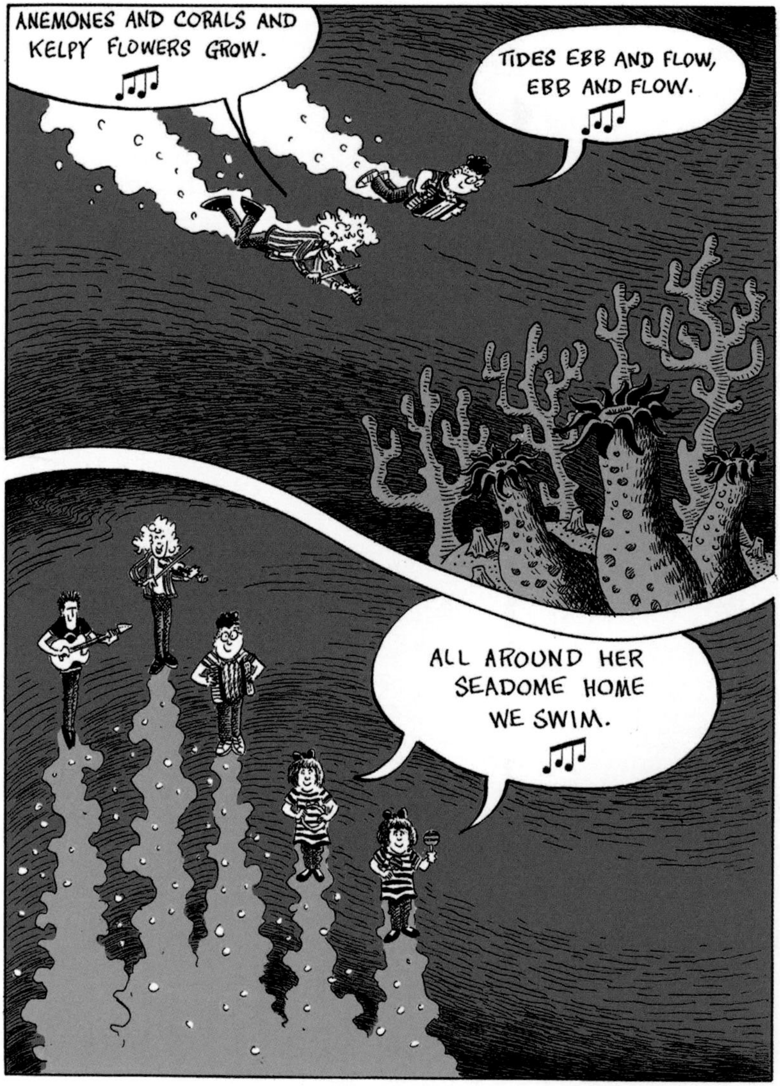
ANEMONES AND CORALS AND KELPY FLOWERS GROW.
TIDES EBB AND FLOW, EBB AND FLOW.
ALL AROUND HER SEADOME HOME WE SWIM.

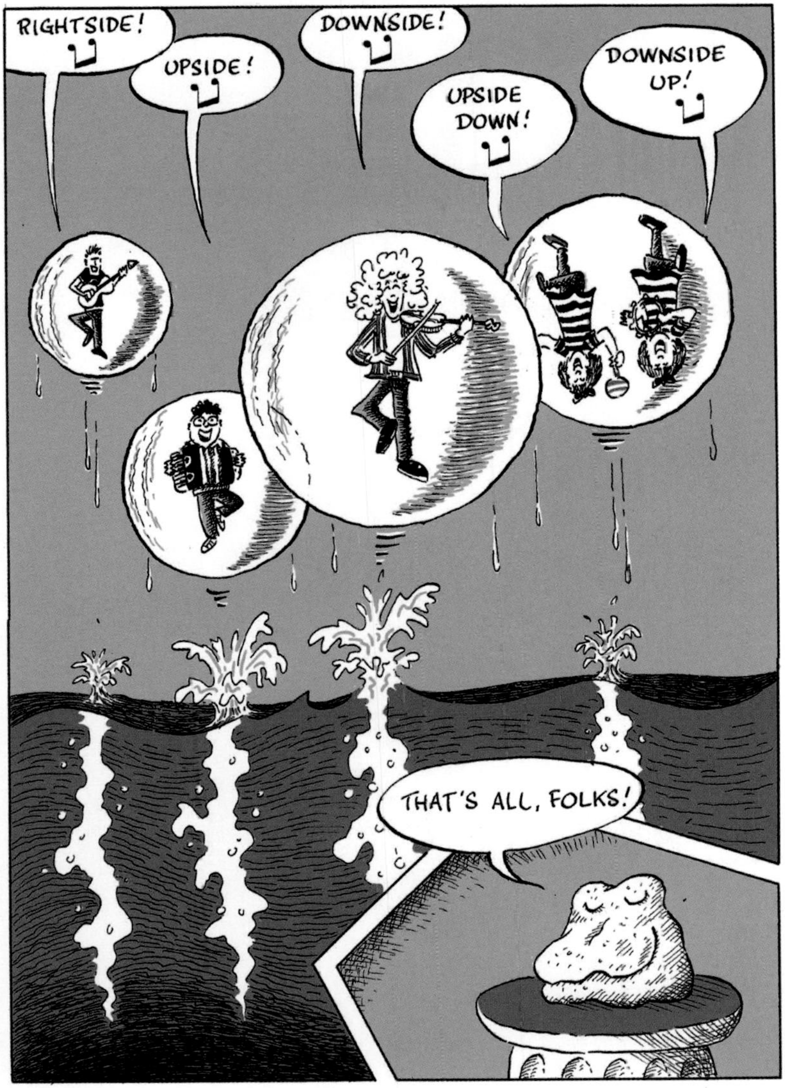
RIGHTSIDE!
UPSIDE!
DOWNSIDE!
UPSIDE DOWN!
DOWNSIDE UP!
THAT'S ALL, FOLKS!

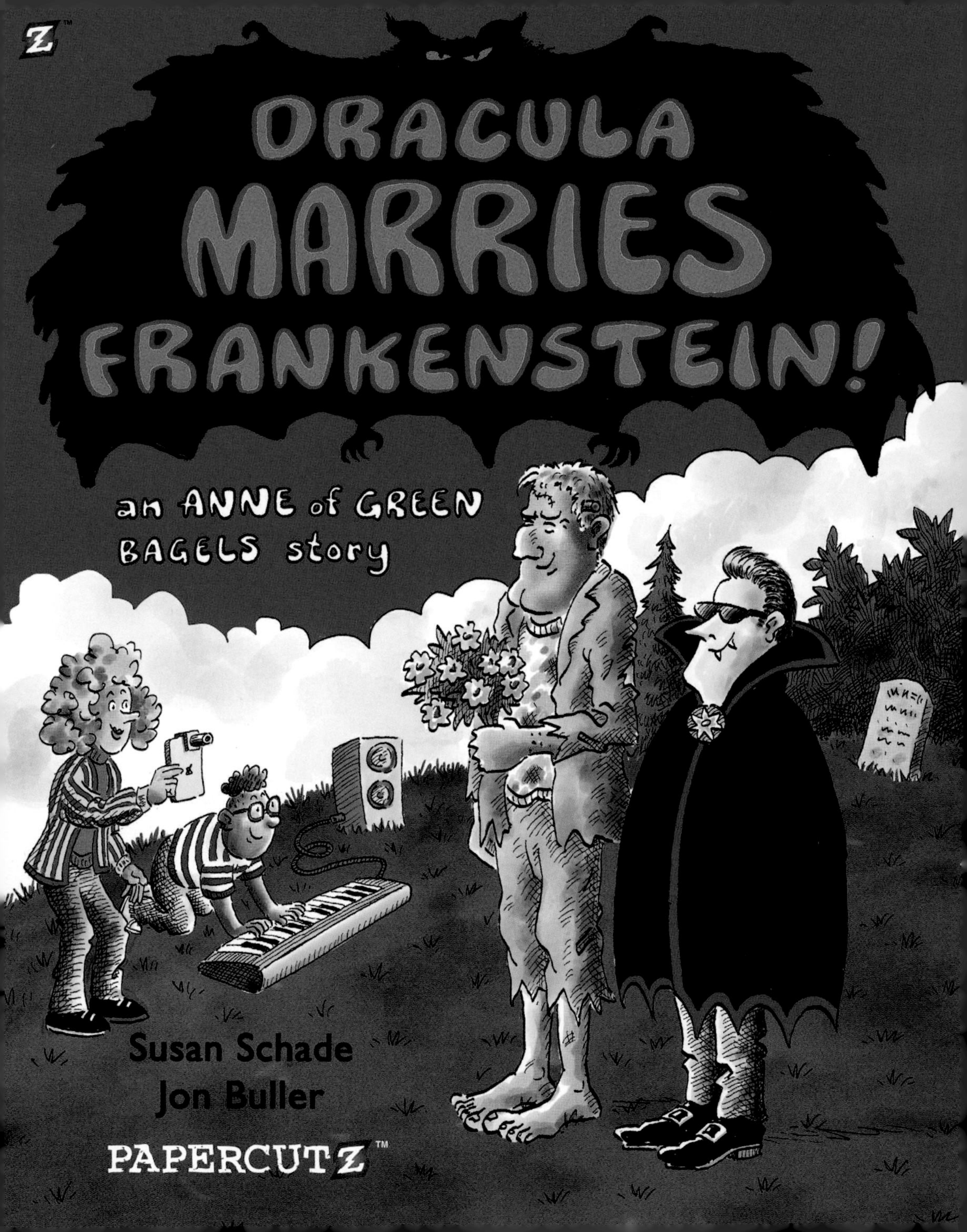
DRACULA MARRIES FRANKENSTEIN!
an ANNE of GREEN BAGELS story
Susan Schade
Jon Buller
PAPERCUTZ

CHRISTOPHER CHURCHMOUSE CLASSICS®

A FLOOD OF FRIENDS

"A man who has friends must himself be friendly"
—Proverbs 18:24, (NKJV).

WRITTEN BY BARBARA DAVOLL
Pictures by Dennis Hockerman

A Sonflower Book

VICTOR BOOKS®

A DIVISION OF SCRIPTURE PRESS PUBLICATIONS INC.
USA CANADA ENGLAND

CHRISTOPHER CHURCHMOUSE CLASSICS

Saved by the Bell
The White Trail
A Sunday Surprise
The Potluck Supper
A Load of Trouble
Rainy Day Rescue
A Pack of Lies
The Shiny Red Sled
A Sticky Mystery
A Short Tail
The Tattletale Tongue
A Flood of Friends

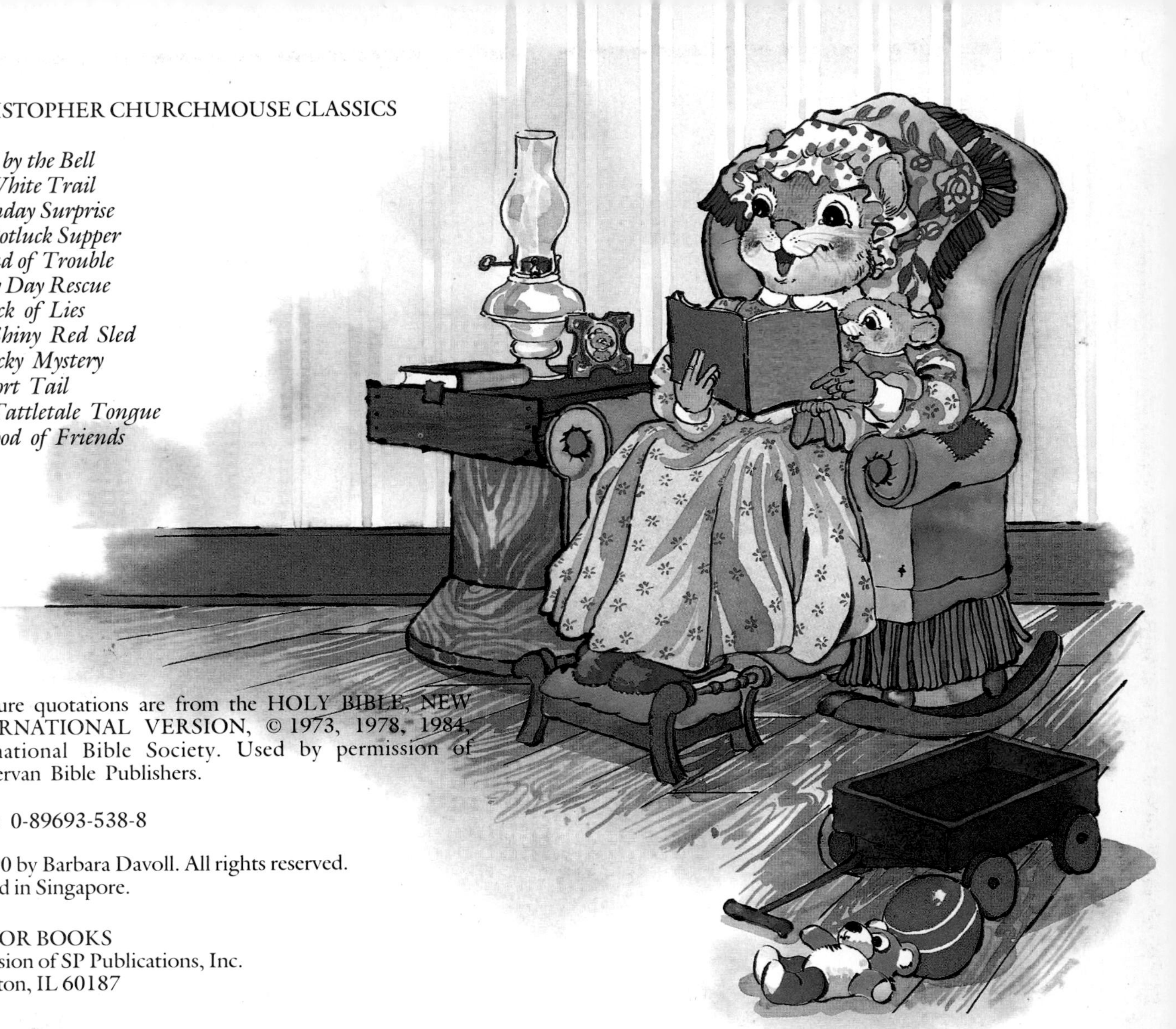

Scripture quotations are from the HOLY BIBLE, NEW INTERNATIONAL VERSION, © 1973, 1978, 1984, International Bible Society. Used by permission of Zondervan Bible Publishers.

ISBN: 0-89693-538-8

Printed in Singapore.

VICTOR BOOKS
A division of SP Publications, Inc.
Wheaton, IL 60187

A Word to Parents and Teachers

The Christopher Churchmouse Series will help children grow in their knowledge of the Lord as they read stories about a delightful mouse and his family and friends.

This book, *A Flood of Friends,* is about friendship and hospitality. God says,

> *"A man who has friends must himself be friendly"*
> —Proverbs 18:24, (NKJV).

This is the story of how Christopher Churchmouse met one of his best friends, Freddie Fieldmouse, and learned how to be a good friend. Freddie, in turn, is a wonderful friend even to an enemy in danger.

The Discussion Starters on page 24 are to help children make practical application of the biblical truth. Happy reading!

Christopher's Friend,

Barbara Davoll

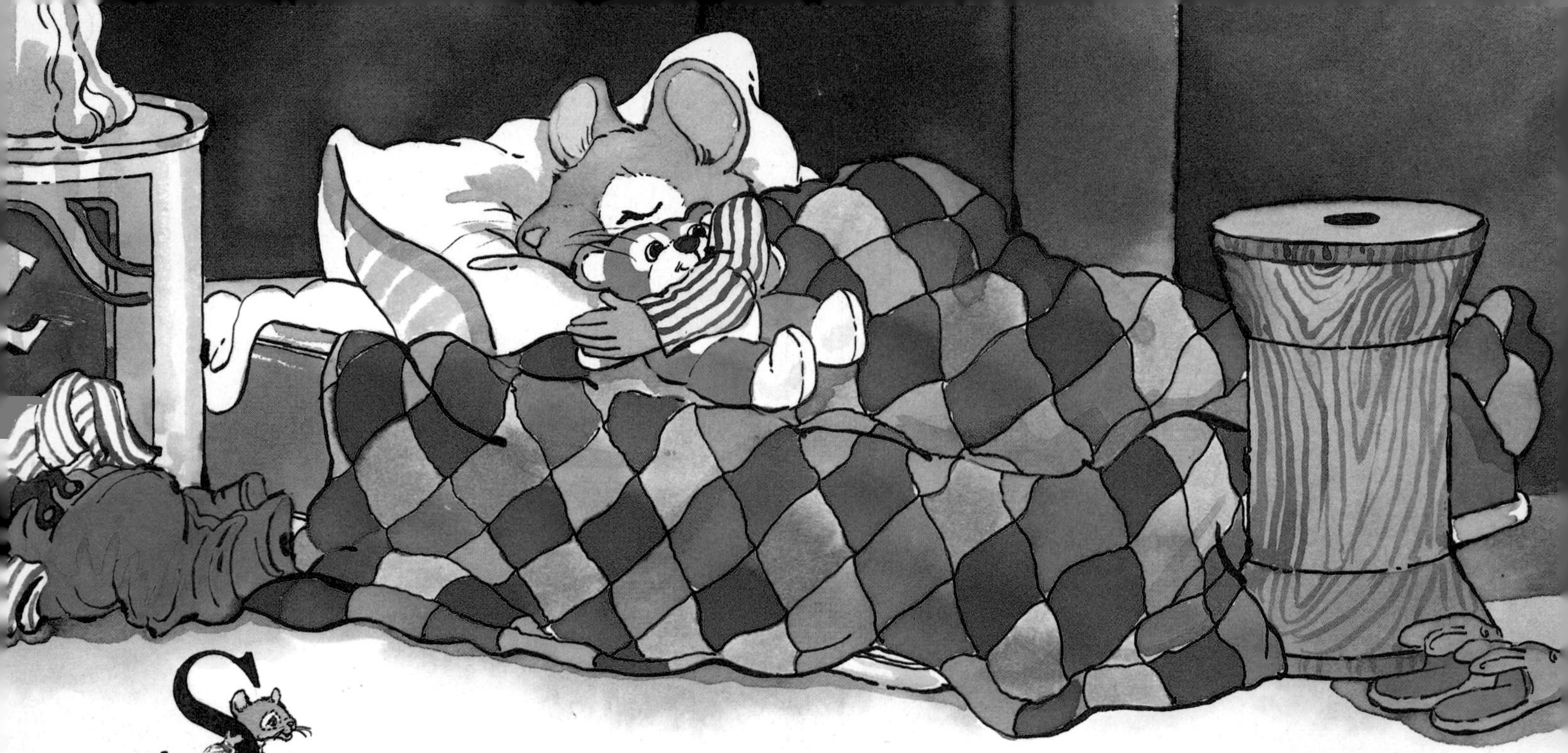

Something was tickling Christopher's whiskers as he lay in bed. "Quit," he squeaked in his sleep. "Oo, don't tickle me!"

Then he opened one eye and giggled. It was just the wind tickling him. He breathed in. Oh, what a wonderful smell—it must be lilacs.

He had just been dreaming of another beautiful spring morning, about this time last year, when something very special happened . . . And this is what it was . . .

It was the nicest spring morning yet. Christopher jumped out of bed and brushed his whiskers and gave his tail a tweak to get the kink out of it. He looked out the window. He couldn't wait to play!

But Sed, Ted, and Ned, his cousins, were away on vacation, and his friend Mandy had to work. As Christopher sadly buttoned the straps on his overalls, he heard Mama Churchmouse. "Come on, Christopher! Breakfast is ready."

Christopher and his mother always had breakfast together, since Papa went to work very early. "Mama," Christopher glumly said as he sat down, "I wish I had someone to play with." He picked up a piece of fruit.

"I wish I could play with you, Dear, but I must go shopping this morning. Mandy's mother is going to take care of your baby sister."

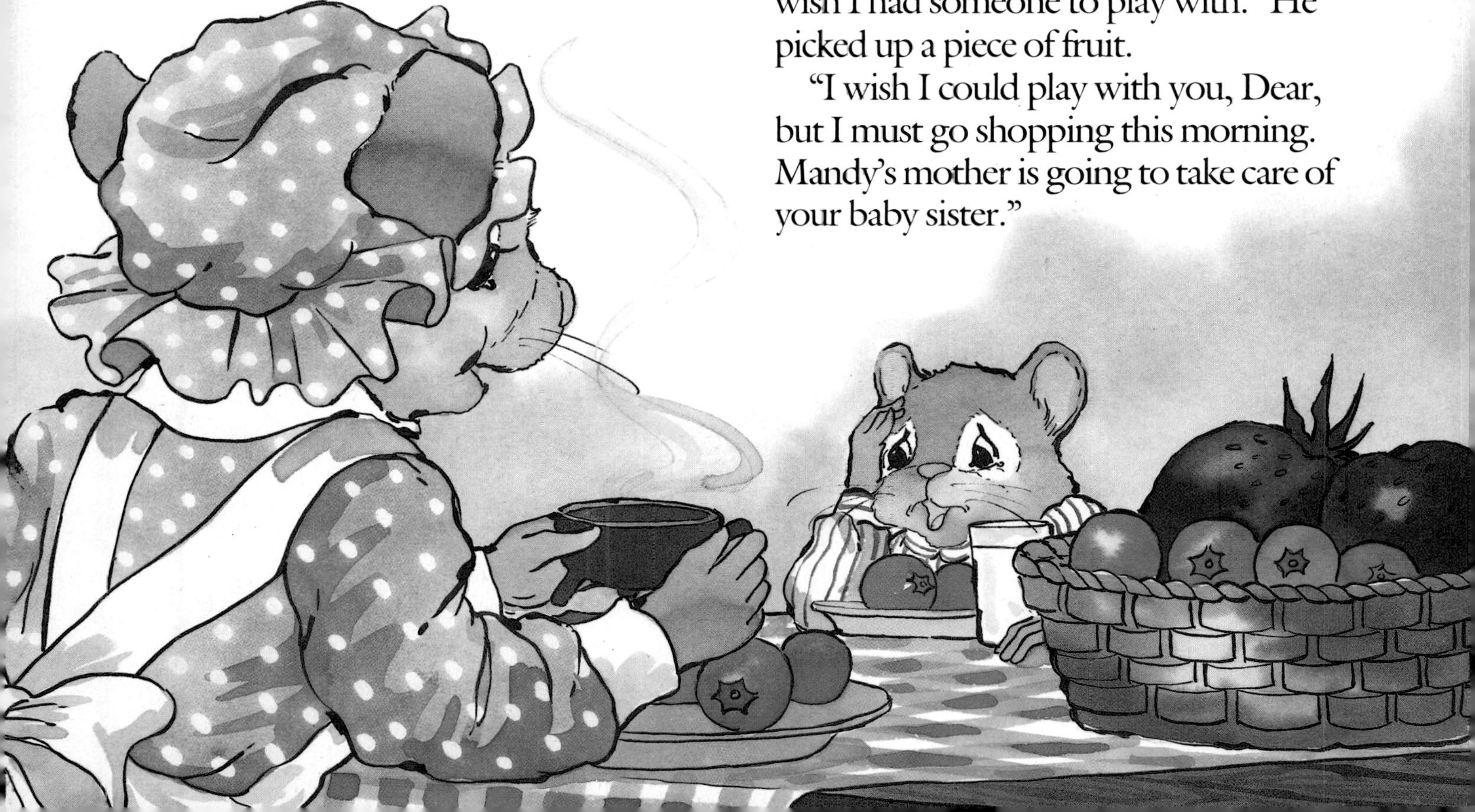

"I wish I had a friend who could *always* play."

"That would be nice. But sometimes it's nice to play alone."

"But, O Mama, I so want someone else today. Where could I find a friend?"

Mama leaned back in her chair. "Well, I don't know exactly *where* you can find a friend—but I do know *how*."

"You do? How?" Christopher asked eagerly.

"The Bible says, 'A man who has friends must himself be friendly.'"

"Why, I'm friendly."

"I think God means *being* a friend."

"Mm. Like being kind? And sharing with someone?"

"Yes."

Chris frowned. "But there's not anyone around for me to be a friend to, Mama!"

"Well, the day isn't over yet!"

6

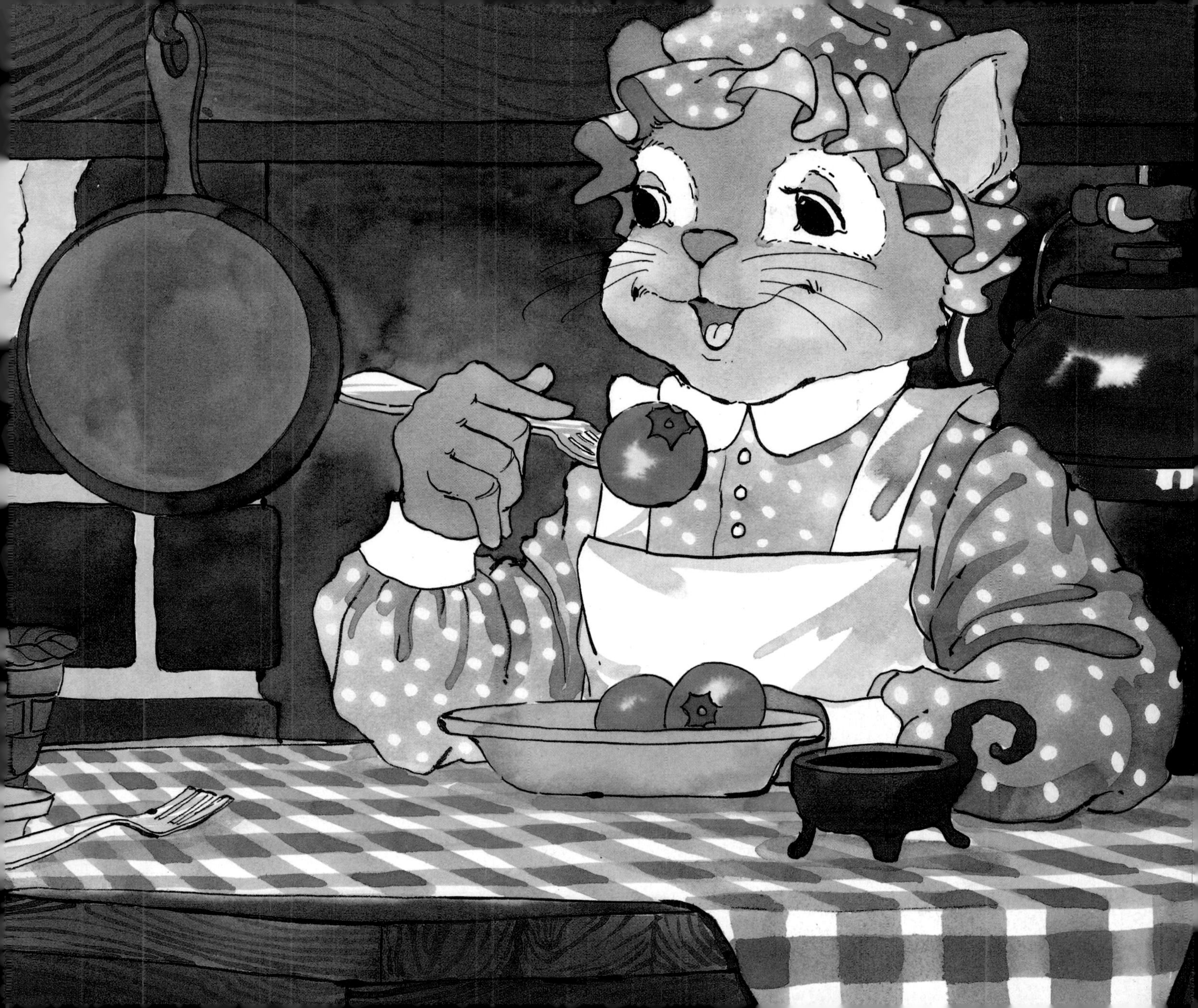

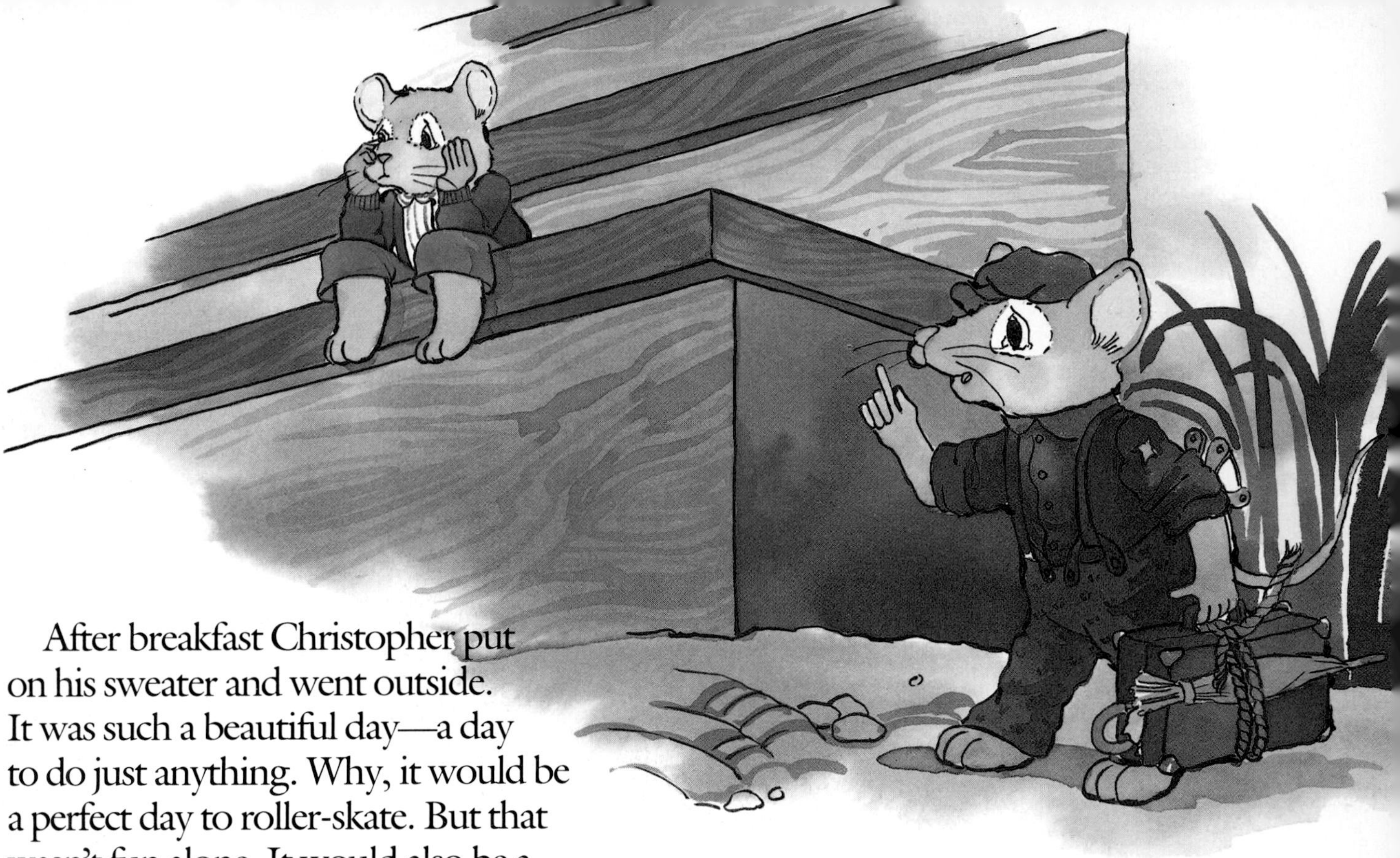

After breakfast Christopher put on his sweater and went outside. It was such a beautiful day—a day to do just anything. Why, it would be a perfect day to roller-skate. But that wasn't fun alone. It would also be a nice day to play ball—*But how can you play ball alone?* Christopher thought gloomily. He scuffed his toes in the dirt. What good was a nice day if you were all alone?

He sat down on the steps of the church in a pout.

"Good morning," said a little voice.

Christopher looked up in surprise. Another little mouse was standing in front of him! "Hello! Who are you?" said Christopher.

"My name is Freddie Fieldmouse. What's yours?"

"Christopher Churchmouse. *I* live here in the church." He looked critically at the strange little mouse. He was very plain looking. His clothes were shabby. He was dusty all over, and in his paw he carried an old, beat-up suitcase with stuff hanging out of it on all sides. "Where are you going?"

"I don't know," Freddie said quietly.

"You don't know!?" squeaked Christopher. "How come?"

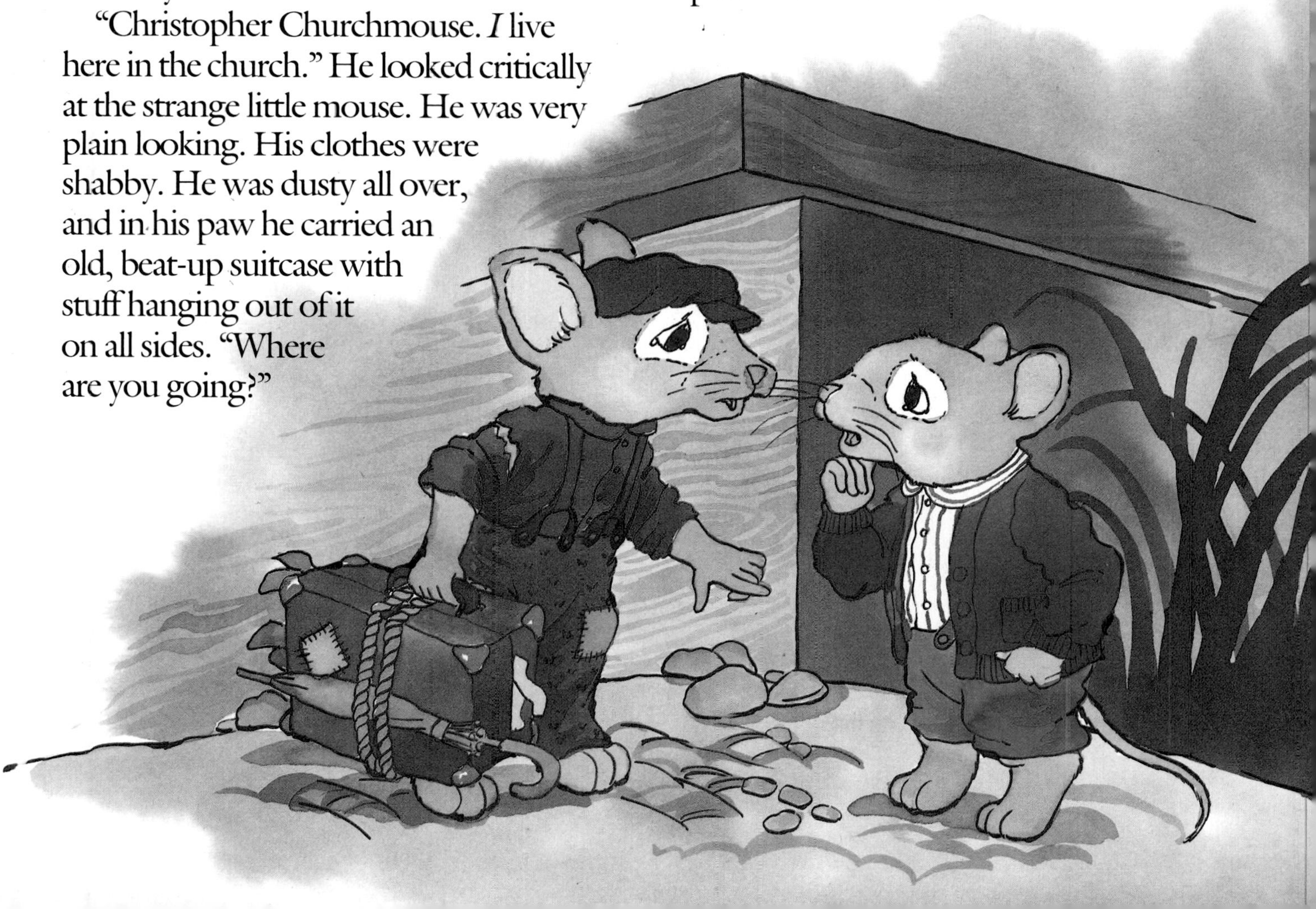

"Well," said Freddie, "it's a long story—but to make it short, I'm looking for a new home. You see, I'm a Fieldmouse from the country—but my home was washed away by spring floods. I need a nice dry home. You don't know of any around here, do you?"

Christopher looked Freddie over again. "Nope," he answered. "Not here. You see, we're all *Churchmice*. We live in the church."

"I see," said the Fieldmouse in a disappointed voice. "Maybe I can find something on down the road. It was nice to meet you, Mr. Churchmouse."

Christopher watched the little mouse trudge down the road lugging the suitcase. *He just wouldn't fit in with us,* Chris thought. Now he could just barely see him, far down the road . . .

Suddenly Christopher jumped to his feet and ran down the road. "Freddie! Freddie Fieldmouse! Wait! Wait!"

10

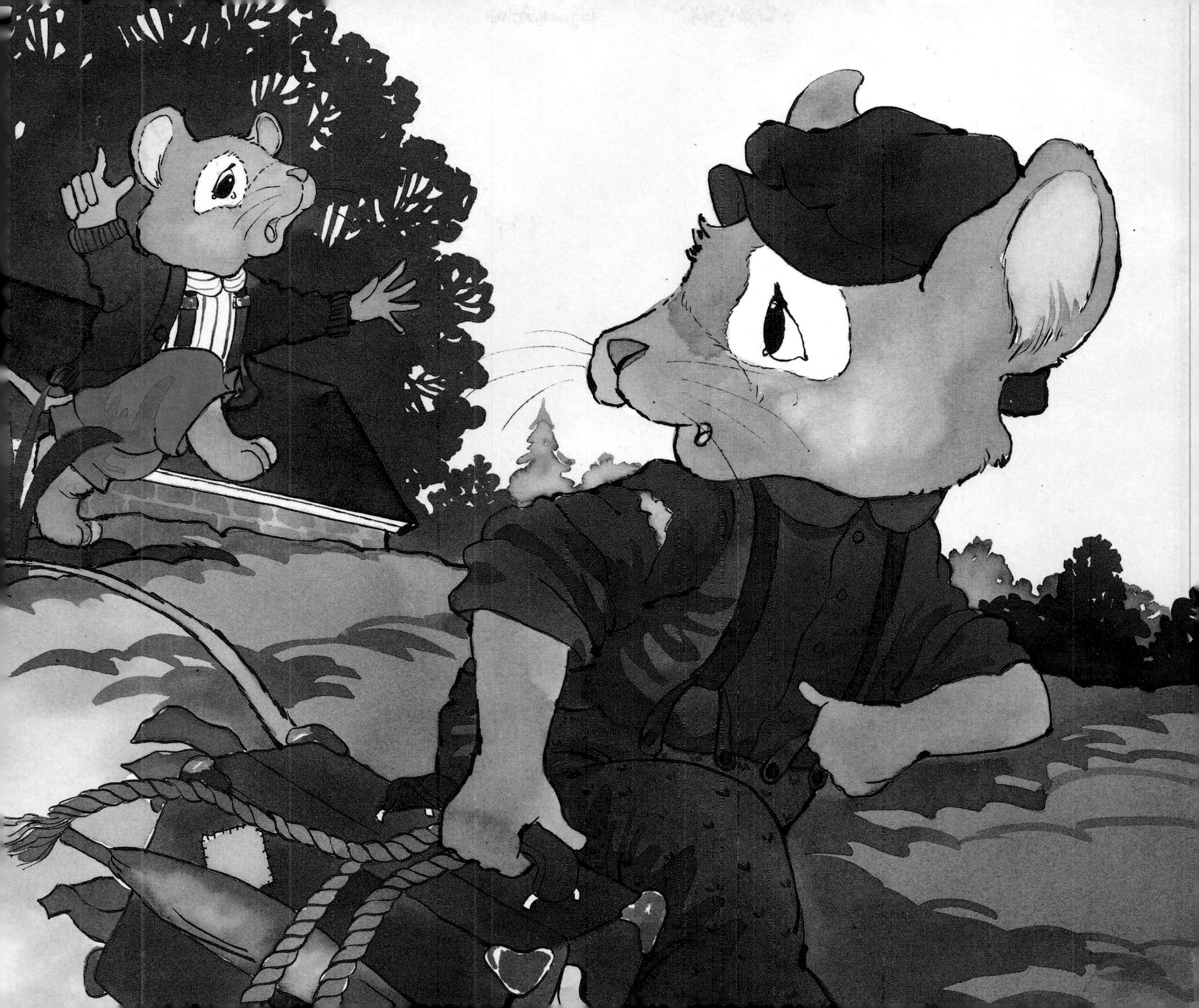

Freddie stopped in the middle of the road. "Freddie," Christopher panted, "I'm sorry. There *is* room in the church. Come on!" He grabbed for Freddie's suitcase. "Let's hurry!"

But Freddie wouldn't let go of his suitcase.

"What's the matter? I said you can come live at the church."

"But—but—wait," sputtered Freddie. "You don't know . . . I didn't tell you . . . I'm not alone!"

"You aren't?" questioned Christopher, looking around curiously to see who was with him.

"No, I'm not . . . Well, at least I won't be. You . . . you see, my family has sent me ahead to look for homes for *all* of us Fieldmice. All of our homes were destroyed."

"Oh," said Christopher in an understanding way. "Well, we probably have enough room for all of you! How many are there?"

"Well, with my Aunt Freda and her ten children, there would be—uh, eighteen, I guess," Freddie said quietly. "I'm sure you don't have that much room—so I'll just be going along."

Christopher grabbed Freddie. "Let's go see my mama, Freddie. She will know if we have enough room. Let's go ask her."

"I—I don't know. I don't want to cause you any trouble. I . . ."

"Come on," Christopher interrupted. "I'm your friend, Freddie,

and I'm going to help you. Let's go!" And with that he took Freddie's suitcase and tugged Freddie along.

Just then they saw Mama carrying her market basket out on the road. "Mama!" Christopher hurried toward her. "Mama, this is my new friend, Freddie Fieldmouse!"

13

"Why, how nice," exclaimed Mama. "Where are you from, Freddie?"

"The country, Ma'am."

"Mama," said Christopher anxiously, "do we have any room in the church? What I mean is—Freddie's home—and his family's—have been destroyed by the spring floods. Freddie's family has sent him ahead to look for homes for them. We have room, don't we, Mama?"

"Why, I'm sure we do, Christopher," answered Mama. "We have an old storeroom that we can turn into apartments very easily. Where is your family now, Freddie?"

"They're coming along slowly with all of the children and mice babies.

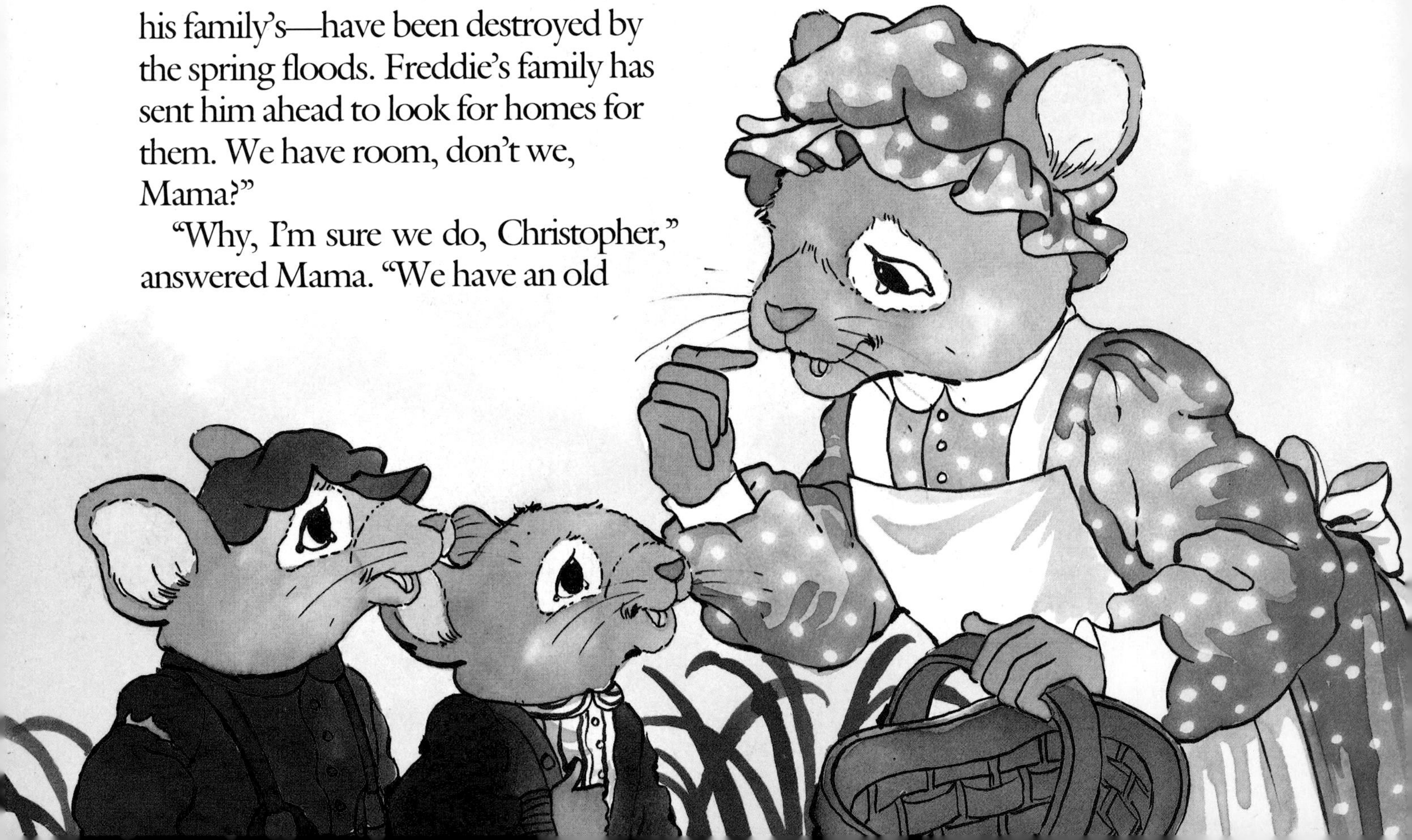

They can't travel very fast."

"Well, we must get busy," said Mama, briskly. "Do you think they will be here by lunchtime?"

"I expect so, but—but you certainly don't have—"

"Christopher, I must go on to the store. You take Freddie home and begin cleaning up that storeroom. I'll be right back and stir up some of my good crumb stew." With a flounce of her skirt, Mama bustled down the road.

The two mice boys worked very hard, sweeping and dusting the old storeroom and carting away some rubbish. By the time Mama was back, it was shining clean. Freddie went down the road to meet his family.

15

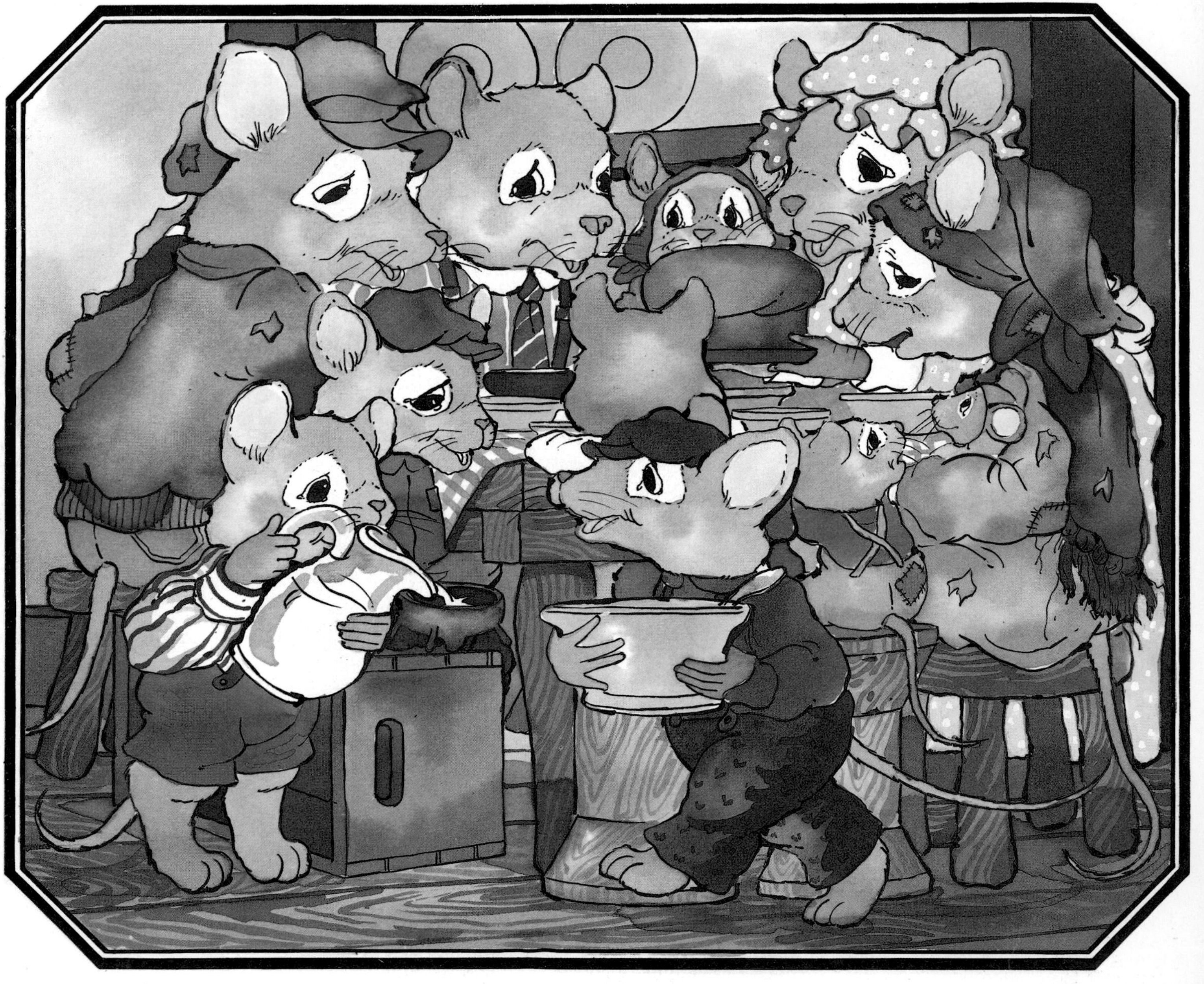

The delicious smell of crumb stew was filling the air when he brought them to the Churchmouse door.

"How can we ever thank you?" said Freddie's father as they were introduced.

"Oh, think nothing of it," answered Mama. And soon all the little children and their mamas and papas were hungrily eating crumb stew. Christopher and Freddie bustled about helping to serve them. Freddie was so happy his eyes were shining. Christopher's face was beaming as he thought of how he now had a whole kitchen full of friends!

The next few days were very busy ones as the Churchmouse family helped the Fieldmice get settled in their new apartments. Then Aunt Snootie and her family arrived back from vacation.

"Are they here?" asked Aunt Snootie, coming into the Churchmouse home.

Mama looked up. "Why, who do you mean?"

"Those pesty Fieldmice," answered Aunt Snootie.

"Oh, no—they're in their own apartments. They're all settled in now."

"Well, I never!" exclaimed Aunt Snootie, peering at Mama through her glass eyepiece. "I can't imagine what has gotten into you, letting those Fieldmice clutter up your storeroom with all their junk, and eat all your food."

"Why, don't you think we should help a mouse family that is in need?" questioned Mama in surprise.

"Well, maybe a *Churchmouse* family, but certainly not *Fieldmice*. They certainly aren't going to freeload on *us*."

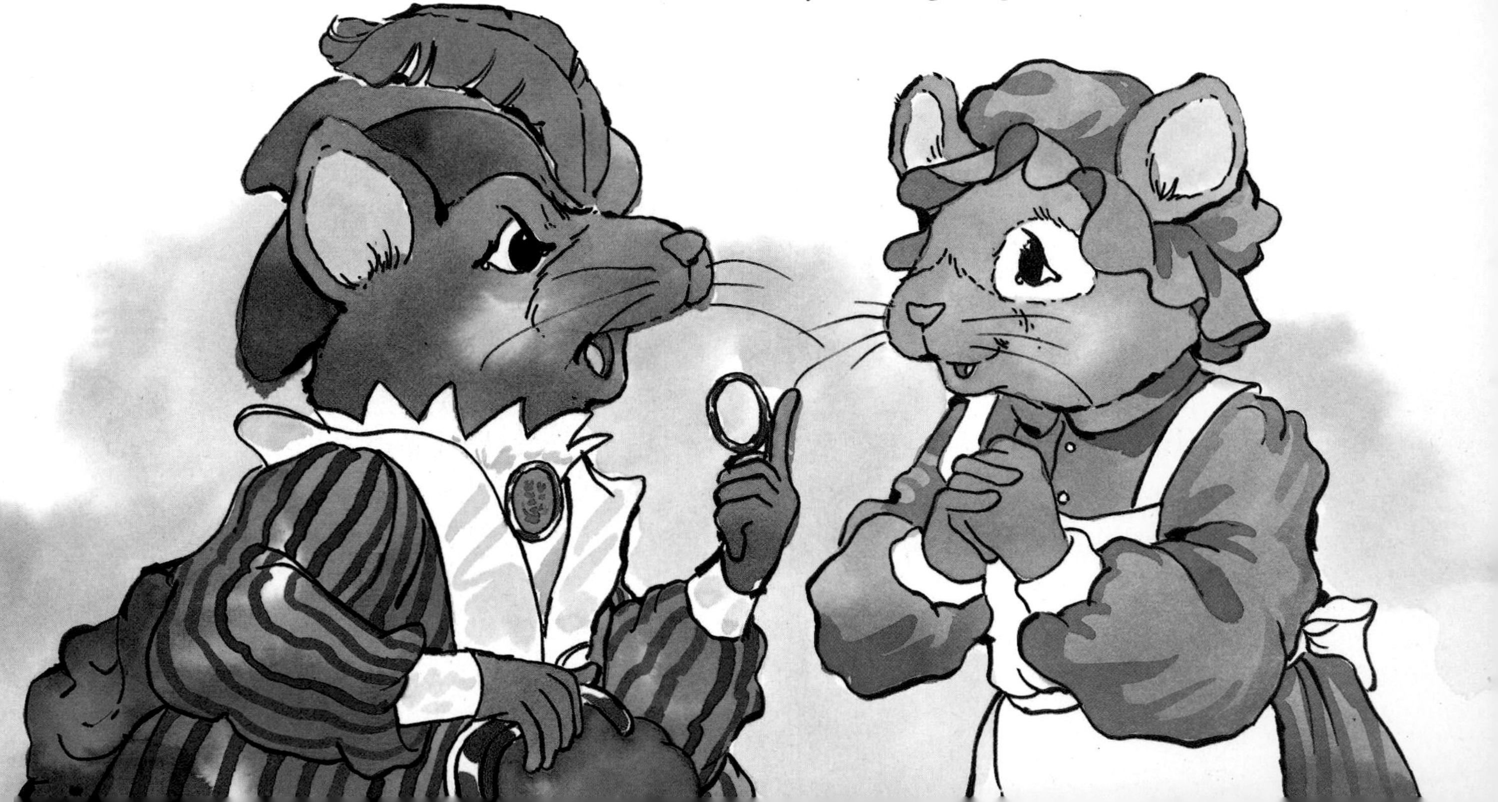

And Aunt Snootie flounced out and slammed the door.

"How sad," said Mama.

One night sometime later, Papa Churchmouse suddenly woke up, knowing that something was very wrong. He sat up sniffing, feeling danger all around him. He carefully put his feet down on the floor—there was water there, up to his ankles!

"Mama! Mama, wake up! Take the baby—there's water all over the floor! You must go to a higher place right away. Chris and I will wake the others."

Christopher and Papa ran all over the church basement, awaking the other Churchmice and Fieldmice. "We must all get up on the steps.

It looks like a water pipe has burst. The whole basement is flooding!"

The church was filled with mice squealing with terror. Christopher helped the grown-up mice swim the mice babies to safety. They held the babies' heads high above the water, then handed them up to their mamas.

Mama Churchmouse was counting all of the mice on the steps. "Papa!" she squeaked. "I don't see Grandpa and Grandma Churchmouse and Uncle Rootie and Aunt Snootie's family!"

Suddenly Christopher realized that Freddie Fieldmouse and his family were missing too. They had been

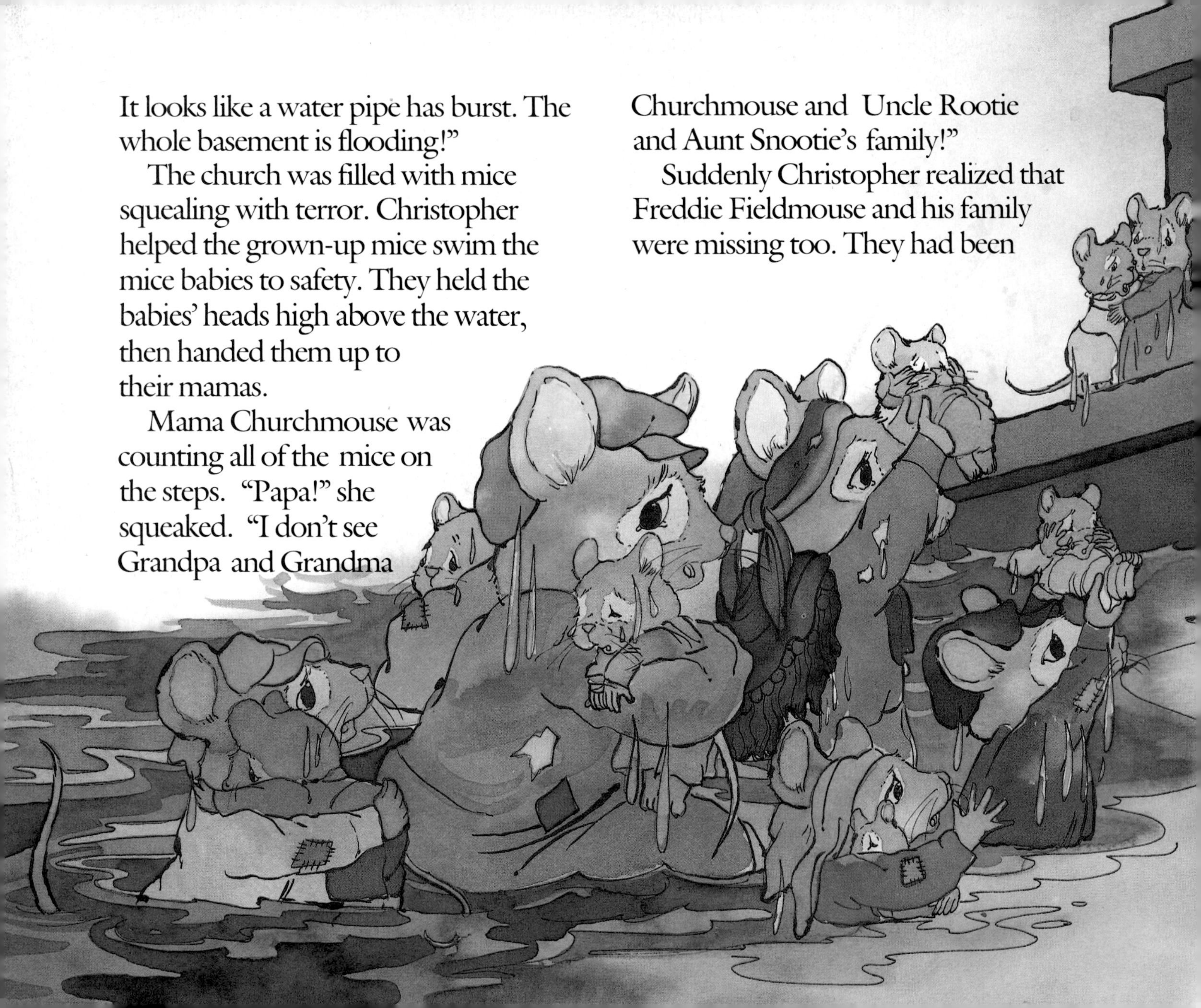

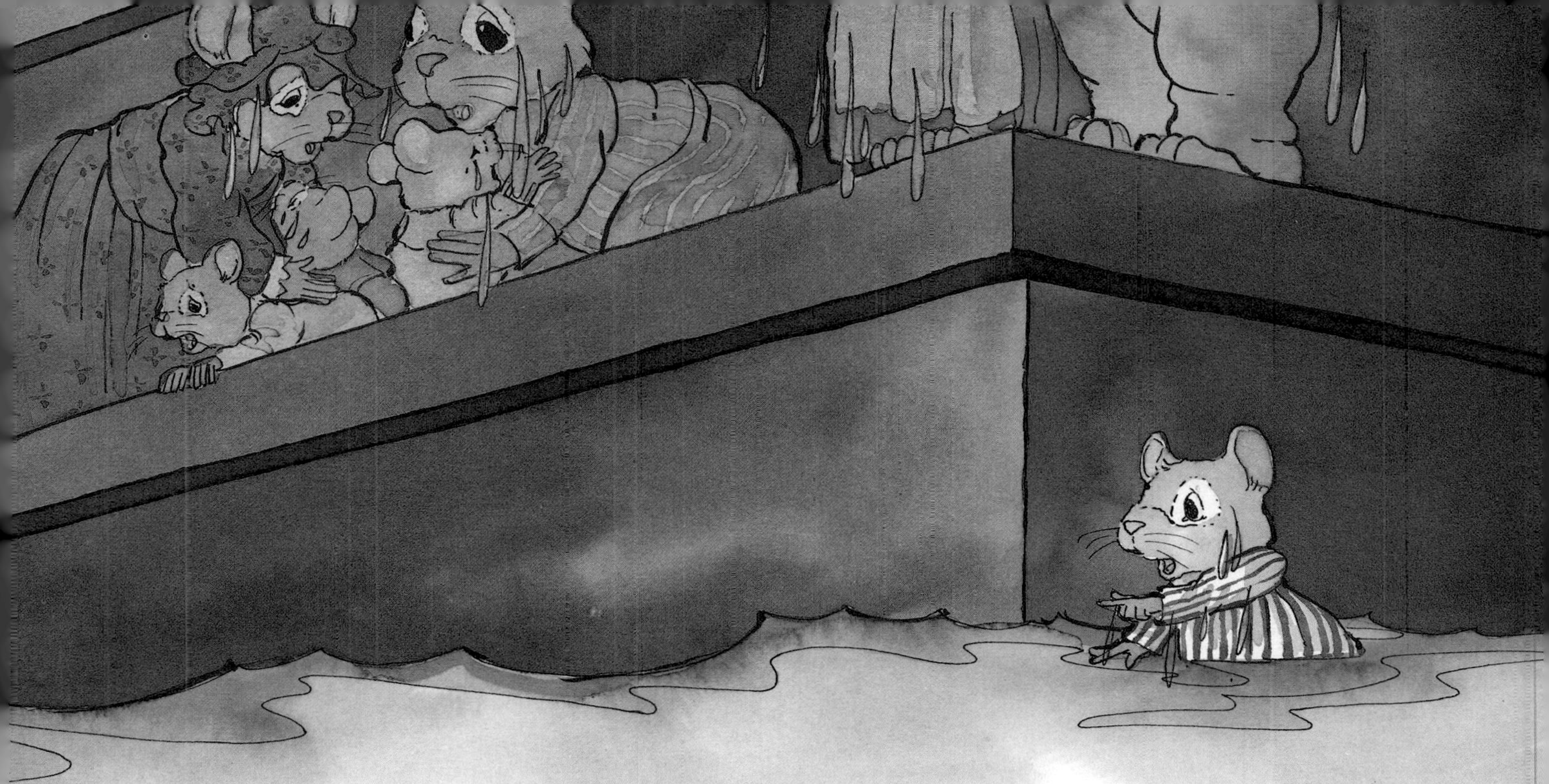

right behind them an hour ago, but now they were gone! And the water was rising!

"Freddie!" wailed Christopher. "Freddie! Where are you?"

But he didn't hear an answer, and he began to cry.

Just then there was a little sound from the water. It was the sound of baby mice crying! Peering around the corner of the stairs, he saw Freddie and his family. Each Fieldmouse had a baby Churchmouse in his paws, holding them high above the water.

And there were Uncle Rootie, Aunt Snootie, and their older children, Sed, Ted, and Ned, swimming in the water! And floating on some small pieces of wood were Grandpa and Grandma Churchmouse.

"Papa! Look! The Fieldmice have saved the rest of our family!" squealed Christopher excitedly.

The mice reached the steps. Aunt Snootie was crying! "But you're rescued, Aunt Snootie," said Christopher.

Aunt Snootie turned around to Freddie's family. "Oh, please forgive me for the awful things I've said about you. I've been—terribly—well—*snooty!*"

At that, all of the mice began to laugh and hug each other. And the Fieldmice never returned to their houses in the country, but they remained in the church, where they had found true friendship.

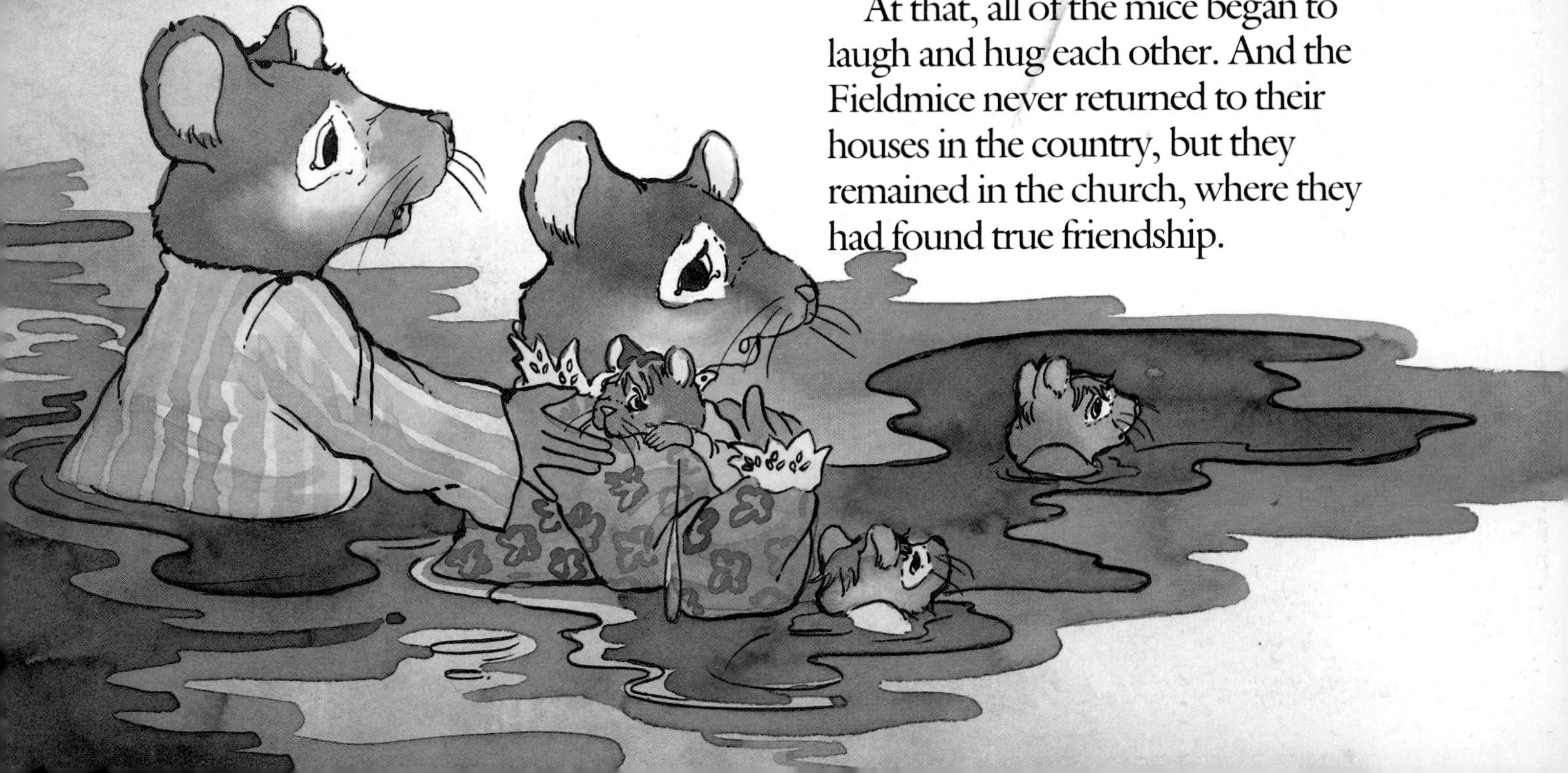

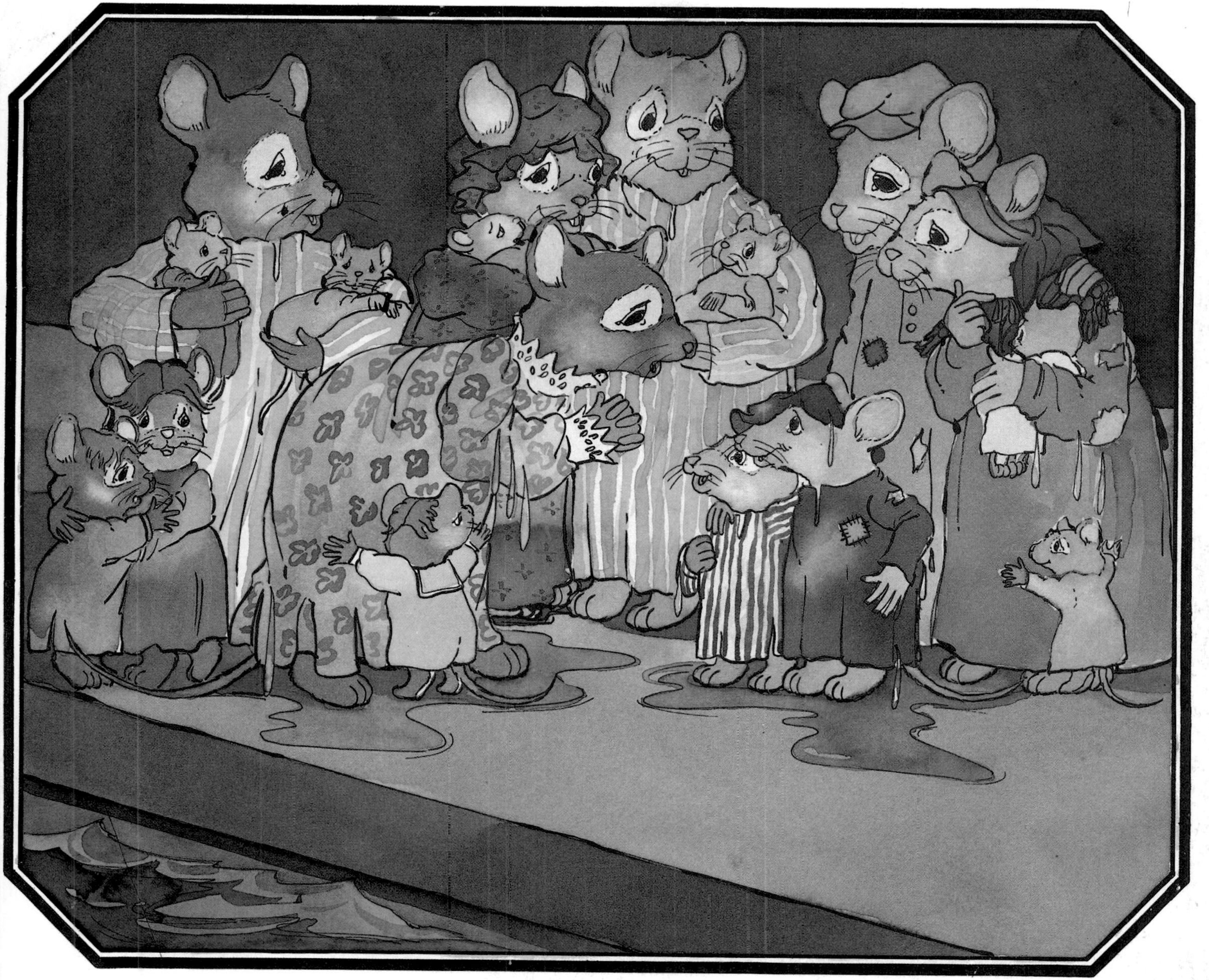

DISCUSSION STARTERS

1. Why was Christopher sad and lonely?
2. How did Mama say Christopher could find a friend?
3. What did the Bible verse mean about being "friendly"?
4. Why did Christopher not want Freddie Fieldmouse for a friend at first?
5. How did Christopher and his family show real friendship for the Fieldmice?
6. What did the Fieldmice do for the Churchmice?
7. Do you have all the friends you want? How can you be a better friend?